Monaco Cool

Monaco Cool
by Robert Westgate

enigma books
silver spring, maryland

Published by:

Enigma Books
An Imprint of Bartleby Press
11141 Georgia Avenue
Silver Spring, MD 20902

Library of Congress Cataloging-in-Publication Data

Westgate, Robert, 1954-
   Monaco cool / by Robert Westgate.
     p. cm.
   ISBN 0-910155-23-2
   1. Westgate, Robert, 1954-   —Homes and Haunts—
Monaco. 2. Monaco—Social life and customs.
3. Americans—Monaco—Social life and customs. I. Title.
DC943.W47A3 1992
944'.949—dc20   92-28027
                                              CIP

Manufactured in the United States of America

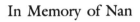

In Memory of Nan

1

I couldn't believe my eyes: a group of French people smiling at *moi*. They weren't real, of course, but the product of a slick Madison Avenue campaign combining imagination with chutzpah, probably conjured up during a cocaine binge.

Yep, the French have taken a beating in recent years, what with terrorist histrionics and a weak dollar keeping we Americans at Epcot.

So now, after decades of openly despising our plaid trousers, loud mouths and bratty kids, they're desperately trying to lure us back with the kind of superficial smiles you find at McDonald's. They are merchandising themselves because they discovered something important: the stark economic reality of life without us. They want us back, all right. More likely, they want our greenbacks.

So they're offering all kinds of special deals; alleged bargains; package tours accented with multiple asterisks and fine print detailing restrictions so severe, you'd be better off buying a regular ticket.

But they went too far when they advertised a full-page color photograph of 16 French men, women and children beaming in my direction—big, warm, inviting smiles, smacking of sincerity, oozing kinship; begging my immediate presence at their friendly open-air café where they could serve me cappucino at five bucks a pop. Understand, I've been to France many times, and I've never seen smiles like that. A pout is the favored expression, except when they see Americans. Then they scowl.

I should have lodged a complaint with the Federal Trade Commission. Instead, I hopped a plane. Not to France, but to Monaco, surrounded by France, on the glamorous Cote d'Azur.

This bout of whimsy was supported by something that happened a few months earlier akin to winning a lottery. Suddenly, I could take a year off from malls and junk phone recordings and hypodermics on the beach.

And this meant I could drop a curtain on my self-imposed exile in New Jersey, to which I had escaped from a family biz in London.

I'd been kicking around in the book business, mostly getting kicked back, but scrounging a handful of five-figure advances as an agent for mostly thankless, haughty clients. Trying my best to be a reformed expatriate.

Commuting to Manhattan, trudging the grimy streets was easy. But Europe kept calling my name. My parents took me on a summer vacation to London that lasted 17 years, and ever since, the concept of home has been elusive. When people ask where I'm from, do I say southern California, where I lived till age 14, but now consider an alien dimension? Or London, where I truly grew up, but whose climate and obsessive class consciousness I have since renounced? Certainly not New Jersey, an extension only of my marriage to a Jersey girl.

I haven't yet found my Bedford Falls. And though I didn't expect Monaco to fill that void, a spot of deviation couldn't hurt; a last hurrah before growing roots some place sensible.

I'd been to Monaco several times in the '80s—a fairy-tale principality nestled between the azure Med and a French Alp, smaller than Central Park, crossroads to the jet-set, lauded by Guy de Maupassant as a "mixture unique on earth." It was this mixture I now craved, plus lots of sun; spectacular scenery. I could see myself donning a white linen suit and Panama hat, cruising a corniche in a convertible, joining the ranks of expat writers.

And when I matched that vision side by side with the robotoid commercialism of New Jersey, enveloped in a quasi-cultural cocoon dominated, no, *intimidated* by consumer extremism and telewave hypnosis, there was no contest. It was time to blow the popstand.

Spontaneity directed me. A friend called to report that a two-bedroom apartment in a building called Le Shangri-La (but of course) would soon become available. Flats like this, at a grand a month, are *not* expensive when you're talking French Riviera and Monaco, for Chrissakes. But they *are* hard to come by. So I grabbed a flight, made a cursory inspection and signed a lease.

My enthusiasm to become part of De Maupassant's mixture and attempt survival in the world's swankiest neighborhood, and the speed with which I enlisted, hardly gave my wife a chance to protest with more realistic concerns: doctors, dentists, a school for our six year-old daughter and the French language, of which we knew seven words between us.

The in-laws saw us off, shedding tears, and we waved goodbye to our neighbors the Dohingers, looking at us out their window, as usual, like a couple of squirrels.

I don't like overnight flights, but you don't have much choice non-stop from New York to Nice. The first half-hour of these oceanic hops is always busy. You say your prayers as the aircraft taxis into position, including Allah for the benefit of the swarthy, moustachioed Arab in the next row in case he has an alternative destination in mind. Then you will the big bird up into God's country, not wanting to meet him this trip, level out, and reward yourself for a job well done with a mimosa or three.

You look at your watch and can't believe 45 minutes have elapsed. But don't kid yourself. The next seven-plus hours are like watching your brother-in-law's home videos— in slow motion. Finding the right position for your back and knees will eventually lead you to a chiropractic.

You stumble off the next morning (2am, to you) looking like a third-string zombie in *Return of the Dead*, hair standing upright like Don King, eyes you want to yank out and run under cold water; atrophied muscles and petrified joints that snap and creak as you chase your baggage around the carousel. Your best Hickey-Freeman looks like it was cut in Bulgaria by a Turkish tailor drunk on Ouzo. Your feet are swollen two sizes larger than your loafers; your brain, one size larger than your skull—and the stewardess wouldn't even give you aspirin.

The apartment wouldn't be available for three weeks, so we set up temporary home at the cheerful, downmarket Hotel Le Siecle, whose one elevator travels so slowly you cannot—this is true—cannot feel it move. The bellboy scratched his head and shoved our nine pieces of over-stuffed luggage after us into a room not much larger than the elevator and hurriedly said *au revoir*. We climbed out in search of cappucino and smiling French faces.

Much later, as we attempted a rearrangement of baggage to create sleeping space, my little girl switched on *the Hypnotizer*, an addiction acquired stateside, and a familiar if unwelcome face appeared, sputtering foreign words.

"I didn't know Alf could speak French!" squealed my delighted daughter.

There we were, no room to stretch, weary, jet-lagged, dogtired, but confident we'd left the lunatic sit-coms behind, only to discover our colonization of the planet is not limited to Big Macs.

I needed REM to put everything into perspective; to quash the second thoughts waltzing madly about my brain. I was into some serious Zs, dreaming about a Pan Am flight home, when an earthquake jolted me from slumberland. The hotel shivered and the earth groaned as a train rolled into the station across the road.

2

Monaco is safe. Real safe. The mugging ratio is on par with the North Pole. The upside is that your wife can walk around at 3am without fear of attack. The downside is, where's your wife coming from at 3am? (A major consideration in Monaco.)

This open-air safe deposit box, less than one square mile of the costliest real estate on Earth, is run like a private country club. If you don't like the rules, you don't join. If you don't know the rules, you will soon, after you've spent your money. And if you *break* the rules, membership is terminated. Forever.

Closed circuit cameras abound—42 of them, strategically placed—and despite open borders with France, its provider, everyone coming and going is scrutinized by the omniscient police force, Carabinieri Control, comprised exclusively—uniquely—of six-foot-tall Frenchmen. It is whispered that there is one cop for every seven residents (it's actually one in seventy). It is whispered that plain-clothes officers (half the force) mingle with residents and tourists, taking notes on idle chatter, and that is why everyone whispers. It is whispered that the police make it their business to know where everyone is bedded at night.

Monaco plays at least part-time home to more millionaires per square foot than any chunk of land anywhere. It's population, just shy of 30,000, is comprised of 90-plus nationalities, with French and Italians predominating and native Monegasques outnumbered five-to-one. There are no beggars, no stragglers, no homeless.

One whispered rule, unwritten except in the minds of its transgressors, is that you don't mess with the natives, or even be *perceived* as messing with the natives. The Monegasque is always right. Period. Next step down is the resident, and after that the non-resident, who has no rights at all.

Let me illustrate:

If a Monegasque has a fight with a resident, the resident becomes a non-resident. If a resident has a fight with a non-resident, the non-resident becomes a non-visitor. If a non-resident hits another non-resident, both Brits get bounced out of town.

Only 15 percent of Monaco's populace work; the other 85 percent are blissfully unemployed, serviced by a workforce of Italians who commute daily by train from Ventimiglia, ten miles to the east.

Nobody cuts coupons in Monaco, and money, is discussed only with your personal banker. If you *don't have* a personal banker, you're probably in the wrong town, but you need only cross the street, to Beausoleil, and exit the fairy tale.

The only snobs are the British *nouveau-rich*, middle-class Brits who have made a bundle, gone tax exile and want everyone to know they've arrived. They're the ones with feigned Oxbridge accents and fancy wheels. Real English aristocrats faint when they see them coming.

The homesick Brits hang out at an English pub called Flashman's, which, to everyone else's horror, has succeeded in importing British meals to France: bangers and mash, egg and chips and other culinary calamities.

* * *

The world's most exclusive small town can be broken down into four villages, each with its own character.

Best known Monte Carlo plays host to the Grand Casino, Hotel de Paris, and Jimmy'z Discotech. Most tourists, knowing no better, stay in the $350-a-night rooms and eat $50-a-*plat* meals within a 500-yard radius of the gambling dens and never stray from the glitz and the glitter.

Monaco Ville a.k.a. The Rock is a genuine medieval village set upon a flat-topped hill of rock bordered all round by a sheer drop. Nature dictated that it be a fortress, and somebody *should* defend it from the souvenir merchants and hordes of Italian sightseers who trample through the faded-pink Royal Palace.

La Condamine. More down to earth than either of the above, the quaint port district buzzes with native color. You recognize Monegasques by looking for signs of dementia in their facial features. Seven hundred years of incestuous in-breeding has produced an exotic people who cross their narrow-set eyes, dribble, exhibit sustained bewilderment and get mad easily. They compensate for being the poorest folk in their own homeland with brazen behavior, like walking into a sardine-packed restaurant without a reservation (essential everywhere) and demanding a table.

"I'm sorry, but we're full," the maitre d' will say.

"You don't understand. We're Monegasque."

"Oh, why didn't you say so? Pierre, tell the noisy Americans at table nine to fuck off, some Monegasques have arrived!"

A village idiot roams Condamine's two main streets, Rue Grimaldi and Rue Princesse Caroline, sometimes blowing a whistle and motioning traffic; a swarthy dwarf scoots around on a midget moped, between your legs if you're not careful; an old bag lady helps herself to fruit and vegetables at the bustling open-air market, clouting anyone who asks her to pay with a wooden stick even more gnarled than she. But don't be fooled: these are Carabinieri Control's three best agents!

Fontvieille. The Principality's newest quarter is built on land reclaimed from the sea. Problem is, the sea is fighting back, evidenced by large cracks in the new apartment complexes and sulphuric odors that breeze by from untraceable places. It is whispered that the Italian architects didn't entirely think things through. The new village some folks call *Funnyville* is slowly sinking.

3

They say tap water is okay, but bowel adjustment to the local *plat du jour* is tough enough without messing with the water, too. You don't discover the meaning of eructation until you eat like the French. The waiter always asks, "Wiz gaz or wizout," referring to the mineral water. But for our delicate American intestinal systems accustomed to homogenized this, pasteurized that and a multitude of chemical additives, the flatulence factor, nature's way of dealing with real food, is at play whichever we choose.

Tiny Monaco is full of itty-bitty shops, itty-bitty restaurants and itty-bitty dog poop liberally dumped by itty-bitty rat-dogs, vicious canines with shark teeth, toothpicks for bones and left over doo-doo stuck to their heiny-hairs. The authorities tried to crack down on these pavement poopers, but for once Carabinieri Control met their match. These temperamental poodles are so pampered in their knitted sweaters and weekly hairdos that they resolutely refuse to do their business curbside. And they do quite an artistic business. Each new poop has a different color and shape, as if these pooches believe themselves French artisans. I saw one poop that stood upright like a miniature ivory tower, waiting for a Gucci loafer to amble along.

The only thing not itty-bitty are the prices. Just order a *citron-presse* at one of the handful of open-air cafés that dot the promenade along the Port of Hercules. A *citron-presse* is old-fashioned lemonade, the kind you used to sell for a nickel on the street, but it is served in so civilized a manner its reward is the fancy name. The *garçon* brings you a glass one-fifth filled with freshly squeezed lemon juice, a jug of water, a spoon and granulated sugar in a glass dispenser. You prepare the drink yourself. This costs two bucks: 50 cents for the drink, and a buck-fifty for the labor, which you did yourself. You think these French are stupid?

But that's a bargain. When my Jeep gets thirsty it costs near 70 bucks to quench it, and you do that yourself, too. No cash discount and positively no green stamps.

You can learn, with practice, to evade dog poop, but there is no way to escape cigarette fumes. The French are tobacco fiends, and their foul, filter-less *Gitanes* release enough nicotine in the air to stain your teeth by proxy.

If you want to see a French maitre'd laugh, ask to be seated in a no-smoking zone.

* * *

I could fit my *trois piece* apartment overlooking the port into my New Jersey living room. This is explained as "The Mediterranean Experience." You live your life *outside* your home.

The realtor takes you for three months' rent, three months' security deposit, ten percent of the total as their fair commission, plus 18 percent tax, and then they take inventory of the *unfurnished* abode, part of a racket called "Keep the Deposit." It is whispered to work like this: when your lease expires they bring over a magnifying glass to assess the wear and tear on the walls, floor and ceiling, then compose a list of hairline cracks and other "damage" and, surprise, surprise! What a coincidence! The cost to restore everything is exactly equivalent to your deposit!

And you can't even sublet. Caribinieri Control is vigilantly protective of Monaco's much-coveted income tax-free address. They are known to make surprise midnight visits to determine precisely who is in residence and bounce from the Principality those who do not jive with the concierge's roster. And never doubt the concierge's loyalty; not to *you*, of course. These are Carabinieri Control's front-line soldiers, watching, always watching, and scribbling little notes into a large book.

To rent an apartment, you have to pay the previous tenant a *reprise*, a quaint French expression for being made to buy someone's old junk. This saves them the trouble of having a garage sale, which is probably illegal anyway. I was forced to buy a combo washer-dryer, an oven and a kitchen cabinet (these are not standard fixtures).

The previous tenant had taken all the light fittings, leaving dangling wires, and no lightbulbs, so I telephoned an electrician and he agreed to come over at 2:30pm. He called that evening at 7:30 to say he couldn't make it.

Next day he finally showed, not at 11:30 in the morning as promised, but seven hours later. Resembling Popeye the Sailor Man, he flicked cigarette ashes on my floor and chuckled as he assessed my predicament, running the kind of meter, no doubt, used by divorce lawyers.

"Zee wire eez too short," he finally pronounced.

"Yes," I said, apprehensively.

"Zee wire eez too *short*."

"*Oui*, I understand," I said. "So what?"

"I will need my tools. You understand?"

"*Oui*, I understand. Why didn't you bring them?"

"*Non*." This was meant to answer my question.

He bid me *au revoir* and mumbled something about *manana*, a Spanish word that assumes special relevance here.

Everyone along the Riviera enjoys a permanently relaxed existence, and you either take Valium and join their pace (the French consume more tranquilizers per capita than any other nationality) or suffer a nervous breakdown trying to get things done double-time in a foreign language.

Business people, too, including bankers, don't care to schedule fixed appointments. They just say to drop by in the morning. When you arrive, they are inevitably tied up with others they've advised to stop in at no fixed hour.

If you arrive past noon, you're too late. The whole coast closes for a two-hour lunch and, time permitting, a round of rootle. And if you don't do the same, you're on your own, ridiculed by those watching you from their open-air tables, laid with vichyssoise, as an uncivilized heathen, obviously American. The movers delivering my newly-purchased furniture dropped everything in the basement garage for two hours, gesturing at me that even thieves, unknown to Monaco anyway, would not operate at lunch-time.

You must reserve in the morning for the weekday *plat du jour* at the *Dauphin Verte* (Green Dolphin), a Condamine café, and you see the same faces at the same tables every afternoon, like one big happy family. It gets so if the guy in the bow tie and turn-of-the-century beard doesn't show, you wonder what happened to him.

The *plats* range from *rosbeef* on Tuesday to a *speciale* on Thursday that often looks and tastes like scrotum stew and, later, provides new dimension to the flatulence factor—and a craving for oatmeal.

In search of pots and pans, snacks and staples, I nipped into the neighborhood *supermarche*. Bang, they hit you for ten francs to rent a shopping cart. The aisles are narrow, like the roads outside, and it's almost impossible not to nail some Frenchie's pooch, and if you do, and they only deport you, you got off lightly. Dogs are sacred to the French; better treated in food markets and restaurants than tourists.

French wine is a bargain; prices for everything else will make you weep. Household items like toilet paper and aluminum foil outprice filet mignon at Safeway.

The French don't like to stand in line, hoping to jostle you out of position by mulling around and inching an elbow into a tight place, say between two ribs; once a wedge is created, they step on your toe; you step back by reflex and, whoosh, they're in front. If you protest, they express bewilderment by blowing a raspberry.

Nobody bags for you at checkout. The pouting cashier dispenses piddly sacks made out of grease paper, the kind that take five minutes to rub open and burst beneath the weight of a six-pack.

The *supermarche*, like every business establishment in Monaco, prominently displays an official photograph of royalty. This is a law. The ubiquitous images of Prince Rainier and heir-apparent Prince Albert slam home the reality of police state-style monarchy, the last of its kind in Europe. This spooks some folks, especially tax exiles, into a low profile. I met two such persons who altered their behavior and professional plans *not* because of an official warning nor even an unofficial tip, but because of a *feeling* that club management may take offense and, God forbid, they would have to seek refuge in Andorra or Campione. Psychological intimidation—glossy 10 x 12s and moving cameras—is enough to keep even the most free-spirited in line.

I suspect Carabinieri Control has devised something they call a Crap Limit, a scale dictating the amount of crap they'll take from you correlated against the size of your balance at a local bank.

Twenty million and they'll let you barf on the street once in a while. Less than a hundred grand and there's not much tolerance. It's *bon voyage* the first time you step on a poodle's tail.

4

After only a few weeks in the Principality, you feel the need to get real, and Monaco is *not* about reality. Travel to other spots in Europe is a large slice of the Monaco experience; coming and going is the favorite hobby of Monaco's non-Monegasque residents.

It's been whispered that the place is so small, so surreal, that "Monaco Fever" sets in after only three weeks of staying put. I lasted two weeks before I knew what they were whispering about; a jaded claustrophobia, like you were living in Disneyland. I had to pierce the bubble, invisible as it was. And there is no finer place to rediscover reality than London.

Always take a raincoat, an umbrella and a pair of rubber galoshes when you visit this incessantly peed-upon city, and throw in a couple of boxes of Kleenex. You can't rely on the trains or telephones, but you can always depend on the rain. And a cold. Not your normal seven-day malady; I'm talking colds that linger: post-nasal drip, catarrh, scratchy throat—a lasting memento to take home and share with others.

The rain falls relentlessly, day and night, four seasons a year. Summer is relegated to ten days in May and three days in October. And even when the sun shines, it's too far away to radiate any heat. The short days and long nights of late autumn are plagued by a damp, penetrating coldness that creeps into your bone marrow and goads it to rebel.

My British Airways Airbus left a spectacular day as it winged its way up and out over the French Alps, then descended through layer upon layer of thick, soggy cloud into London's Heathrow Airport. A hiker's haven, you can easily clock three miles at Heathrow without getting anywhere, least of all an exit. Their strategy is to wear you down so you don't mind standing in a long queue at Immigration while four of the five officers on duty enjoy a tea break, their sixth since starting the day. You've heard of the work ethic? In Britain it's called "work to rule," and work is *not* the operative word.

A turbaned Indian sikh stamped my passport, evidence that the colonies have imploded except in the minds of most Brits, who still talk about a sun they never see never setting on a supposed empire.

I walked out the terminal and my breath immediately vaporized as I exhaled. The dampness grabbed me, invaded my body, and I could actually feel myself becoming unhealthy and pasty-faced.

London cabbies are an engaging lot, and this is good because there is loads of time for discussion. The only thing more relentless than the rain is the traffic, inching forward, snarling at roundabouts, gridlocked at intersections—and you haven't even left the airport.

The first thing you notice at your hotel is that everyone has a cold. The check-in clerk, who says your room isn't ready, the bell-hop, who disappears when it is, and most of the guests are starting a cold, in the middle of one or recovering from one and preparing for another. And one thing is certain: you, too, will cultivate a cold within the hour, courtesy of the trillions of germs everyone is so generous about sharing. They sneeze, hack, sniffle, cough and blow their swollen pink noses, always, seemingly, in your direction.

My Knightsbridge hotel room was not worth writing home about despite its hefty price tag, but that's London in a nutshell: not much for a lot of mozuma. The room smelled musty and damp. No, it didn't just smell musty and damp, it *felt* musty and damp. In England, the words "charming" and "quaint" are euphemisms for musty and damp. If we dare complain, we are sternly informed that it is our attitude that lacks. And they are never surprised by attitude-lacking Americans.

I picked up the 'phone in my room to make a call; the line was dead. And when I went down to report the fault, a porter said, "Oh, no, sir. It's not *your* telephone. It's the hotel *switchboard* that's broken down."

"Oh, in that case it's all right," I said. And he agreed.

An old friend joined me in the lounge and I asked a passing bellboy about ordering coffee and buttered toast. He never returned. Then I flagged the attention of an assistant manager and he promised to have our refreshment sent out. Twenty minutes later we were still waiting and, passing again, the assistant manager expressed surprise that we hadn't been served.

"I'll go see what happened," said he.

Ten minutes later he returned with lukewarm coffee and stale scones, explaining that "the bloke in the kitchen has disappeared."

If Hemingway had spent his early years in London instead of Paris, his memoir of that era would have been titled *A Stable Fast*.

It didn't take me long to fit in. My eyes reddened and

grew heavy, my nose was runny and my ears began to buzz. I joined ranks with everyone else and tried to kill the bug with whiskey. That's what the pubs are for, five on every main street.

The pubs compensate for the cold and damp outside by cranking their heating system to full whack and your mucous membranes turn from runny to stuffed-up in two seconds flat. Another 60-seconds and your sweater absorbs a roomful of pipe smoke.

All summed up, this is what invariably happens within a day of arriving in London: you catch a cold, drink too much and finish up smelling like a stale cigar butt. And you are also hungry. Unless you were stupid enough to eat the food, in which case the pain in your gut has nothing to do with cold symptoms. The Brits, with their stiff upper lips, accept food poisoning as a natural risk when dining out. A deeply reserved people, it is against their nature to kick up a fuss, and this ensures that they are badly fed.

You walk into a restaurant, bustling with business, and you think the food *must* be good...until the inedibles arrive: rubbery spare-ribs, precooked last month and nuked in a microwave, french fries boiled in Brylcream and cole-slaw aged pee-yellow.

The worst food of all is to be found in the stuffy, mahogany-lined clubs of St. James's. They dot Pall Mall and collectively form the last bastion of the British Empire. The rhubarb brigade in residence take afternoon tea and still speak of India and the U.S.A. as if they were colonies, and they fondly reminisce the days when Britain prospered by importing everything and exporting nothing. It's different these days, even if their chief export is soccer hooligans.

I hailed a passing taxi and told the driver I wanted the Houses of Parliament. "Too far, mate," he spat, and sped off.

They have more pubs inside Parliament than I have fingers. My old friend Nigel, a lobby correspondent, took me to one for a quaff of whiskey to "kill the cold," and this had the added benefit of killing my taste buds in time for lunch: steak and kidney pie, heavy on the kidneys, canned peas and steak-fries bloated with grease. The only way to swallow this grub is with a dozen gulps of wine, followed by a schooner of port, followed by a brandy—a typical preparation for an afternoon's voting on legislation. The *serious* drinking commences later on, before dinner.

* * *

Checking out, I asked the hotel cashier to deduct the stale scones from my tab.

"Why didn't you let us know about the scones at the time?" She eyed me suspiciously.

"There was nobody around to *tell*, though I hardly see how that changes anything."

"Well, you didn't say anything at the time, so I'll have to take it up with the management."

"You can take it up with your mother if you want. I'm still not paying for stale scones."

In her eyes, I was, doubtless, just another attitude-lacking American in want of manners.

The British begrudgingly serve you, badly, with inferior wares, then lecture you for complaining. Because in Britain, the customer is always wrong. When you walk into a hotel, bar or restaurant, the staff think they're doing *you* a favor. It's not, "Thanks for coming in, chappie, we appreciate your business" but "You think our glasses are dirty? Who needs you anyway!"

The two biggest selling items in Britain are Guinness

beer (five million bottles a day) and Heinz Baked Beans (four-to-six million cans a day). Knowing this, everything becomes clear.

5

E ven *leaving* London is a pain in the dokus. The fog thickened into split pea soup as my Indian cabbie raced toward Heathrow, believing the faster we went, the less time we'd spend at risk on a perilous motorway with ten-feet of visibility.

The airport, engulfed in dense fog, was a madhouse: no runway traffic meant a pile-up inside. I was among 25 anxious passengers waiting for Air France to open its counter for their 9:55 to Nice, though the ground crew wouldn't take our luggage until a London-bound flight from Paris, our aircraft, had landed. And *nothing* was landing.

I sat on my garment bag and read a paperback while rumor swirled 'round that the Paris flight had diverted to Gatwick; logic dictated that we would follow. And though the smaller airport was 50 traffic-tied, foggy miles away, this news came as a blessing because at least we would be headed *somewhere*.

After trudging half-a-mile, luggage laden, to a designated bus and stowing our own bags in its hold, an Air France representative climbed aboard with another announcement:

"You will not go to Gatwick after all, heh, heh. A little mistake. We're going to put you on a flight to Paris, where you'll catch a connection to Nice."

We should have known then and there we were being conned. Airline personnel will send you anywhere and turn you into someone else's headache.

The Paris flight was already boarding so we were urged to speedily reclaim our luggage from the bus, trot a half-mile back to the check-in desk, then fight our way through an airport gone nuts. The fog had thinned and the airlines were in a race to get their delayed flights airborne.

It was bright and sunny in Paris and another Air France rep met our ruffled Nice-bound contingent at the arrival gate. This is where we learned that the promised 3:45 connection would depart *not* from Charles de Gaulle Airport, where we had just landed, but from Orly, the other side of Paris.

A mad dash tempered by Parisian traffic, on a bus; the rep stayed behind, having done her bit.

The bus driver careened to a halt in front of Orly and we disembarked—a tired, angry group of 25 men and women—in search of our promised connection to Nice, scheduled to depart in less than 20 minutes. There was no evidence on the departure board that such a flight existed, so we surrounded an Air France information booth and everyone shouted questions at once.

"Ah," said the puzzled information clerk. "Zat flight does not leave from zis terminal. It departs from Orly *Ouest*"—he checked his watch—"in 15 minutes." He blew a raspberry to emphasize the time.

"Orly *Ouest*?" several of us shouted in unison. "Where the hell is that?"

"Over there." He pointed out the picture window in the direction of a smaller terminal about a mile away.

"The fucking bus driver left us here!" screamed one English lady, stiff upper lip softening somewhat. "Are you people nuts?"

This was a question that begged to be asked, even if I already knew the answer. *They* weren't nuts. *We* were nuts for going along with their cockamamie scheme in the first place. And if we—real walking, talking, living beings—were having this much trouble, God knows how our luggage was faring.

Now, in life you find that out of adversity springs friendship, and it was at this precise moment we passengers abandoned the code of strangers and conspired to take matters into our own hands, reasoning that we'd be better off *without* assistance from Air France. We would simply fight our way to the connection, protocol be damned.

I and two others—an Iranian and a Scandinavian—led the charge back to where the bus was parked. A few sharp words in four languages were exchanged and we effectively commandeered the bus and driver.

We stormed into Orly *Ouest* and, with eight minutes left, raced around the terminal searching for the right gate. If you've seen *It's a Mad, Mad, Mad World*, that was us.

There it was, *Porte 1.0*, and we rushed breathlessly to the desk. The stony-faced Frenchman looked up, sniffed disdainfully at the huffing and puffing before him, and said simply: "This flight is full."

That's when things turned ugly.

The Iranian let fly a torrent of invective so awesome, we applauded. Frenchmen usually respect this, but *this* Frenchman and his Algerian assistant were unmoved and pretended to know nothing of our plight.

In 25 voices, we loudly, profanely demanded that the highest ranking Air France executive make himself known so we could introduce his head to his colon. Otherwise, we'd start taking innocent hostages.

The two men behind the desk grew nervous and threatened to call the police.

"Throw us in jail, you morons!" we chanted.

An audience gathered. Then a few boarding passes magically materialized and were slipped quietly to the most vocal among us, myself included. Their strategy was brilliant: get rid of the ringleaders; the passive types can wait another six hours.

The plane was packed full of French chain-smokers, all sore at us for holding up the flight, but we returned their glares with equal intensity.

Awaiting our luggage at Nice (it had found another plane), I hit the airport bar with Bhaman, the Iranian, to curse London fog, Air France and ourselves for not having had the presence of mind to hijack the first, Paris-bound flight.

Then came my first brush with French officialdom. As soon as he saw the painting I carried, wrapped in brown paper, the Customs inspector decided I would be living proof that he hadn't slept through his entire shift.

He asked me how much it was worth and, like a fool, I responded honestly, about a thousand dollars.

This was a mistake. You are not supposed to be honest with French Customs. You are supposed to say, "What? This piece of pig-poo? Your mother wouldn't hang it over her pissoir." And they'd believe this because it was painted by an English artist.

Bhaman turned around and decided that this was going to be his *cause celebre*.

"You *stupid* man!" he shouted at the inspector in French. "You *illiterate* farmer! My friend didn't even *have* to walk through Customs with his picture. They cleared it in Paris. Let him pass you stupid fool!"

I thought for sure they'd let me go and take Bhaman into custody. This would have been okay since Iranians enjoy martyrdom.

But they took his abuse and stuck with me.

Bhaman wouldn't quit. He made some more noises and followed up with several obscene arm gestures. More Customs inspectors arrived. They solemnly beckoned me into a small room nearby, lest I try to escape, and closed the door in Bhaman's face. The Iranian's mug appeared at a window, tongue stuck out and thumbs planted in his ears, fingers waving madly. What had I done to instill such loyalty? More likely, the day had been too much for him, and I doubted, in his present state, he could remedy my situation.

The inspectors searched my bags and gleefully uncovered two smaller paintings. They jumped up and down, wore severe expressions and gave me the third degree.

Goddamn, it was good to see someone finally cracking down on paintings.

"Look," I said to one of the new arrivals. "I've been traveling since seven this morning and jerked around all day by Air France. If I've done something wrong, just tell me what it is, and let's settle it before that guy out there drops his drawers."

"Okay, *bon*," he said. "There are two solutions. The first is that we take your paintings and give you a receipt. We will have them valued and after you pay a tax you will have them back."

"Fine," I said. "What's the other option?"

"There isn't one," he replied.

I took a receipt and Bhaman drove us back to Monaco in his pale yellow Rolls Royce.

6

The electrician still had not returned, so I called him to say someone else would do my lighting.

"What about zee equipment I ordered?" he asked.

"Cancel it. If there's a penalty or freight charge, I'll pay it."

He wasn't thrilled about this because—I later discovered—he was due to land a whopping 25 percent commission on my order. So instead of trying to cancel the gear, he beat a path to the supply shop and paid cash in full, then called to say the deed was done.

"Listen," I said, "I've been patient with you since the day we first spoke. But you've messed me around, not showing up, not calling, nothing. I ask you nicely to try and cancel the lights, and what happens? You run out and buy them..."

"So you've found anuzzer electrician?" he asked, incongruously.

"What I've done isn't what's at issue here. It's what *you haven't done*: my lighting. I'd like to talk to the shop myself. May I have the receipt to refer to?"

"Ah, but that is impossible." A Frenchman's favorite English phrase. "My accountant has it."

"So ask your accountant to send it to me."

There was a pause.

"Some of us have to work for a living," he grumbled.

"What? I'm sorry if you don't enjoy your work..."

"Zee 'aves versus zee 'avenuts," he cut in.

"I'm finished doing business with you," I said. "Send me a bill and I'll respond accordingly."

"Oh, it won't be *me* who'll send it," he said sinisterly, "but you'll get it." And with that he hung up.

The silly man 'phoned back a minute later.

"What do you want me to do wiz zee lights?" he asked.

"Do whatever you want with them."

"I'll leave them wiz your concierge."

"Do whatever you want with *your* lights," I said.

"I've been here ten years and I know a few people in zee high places," he snarled.

"Yeah, well I've been here six weeks and I've probably *irked* a few people in high places," said I. "But I know everyone in all the *lowest* places who get high."

"Huh?" he said. "I'm going to the police."

The next call I had was from a bailiff, threatening to confiscate my Jeep. Then the bailiff called Monsieur Molass, the proprietor of Hotel Le Siecle where I keep a room as an office, and asked him to have a word with me about my unwillingness to pay bills. Gross intimidation, but I had already established a good rapport with the Jordanian hotelier.

"I have rights," I told Molass. "I'm an American."

"You have no rights," said Molass, who had once, himself, been stung by the bailiff. "This is Monaco."

"You mean they can take my Jeep?"

"They can take anything they want."

Molass attempted to arbitrate with the electrician on my behalf, grew more perplexed than I, and just when we thought we would have to barricade ourselves inside his hotel, Molass discovered that Popeye did not possess a *fond du commerce*, a business license. Confronted with this gem, enough to get him bounced from the Principality, Popeye conceded defeat, and we never heard from the bailiff again. Carabinieri Control conveyed *their* opinion on the matter by erecting a large, lighted sign outside my front balcony that said *SCHLITTENFAHRT*. That's what I *thought* was going on until I looked down and beheld a German gypsy fair stretched from one end of the port to the other. The *Schlittenfahrt* was just an Alpine ride that goes 'round and 'round and up and down, simultaneously, at a hundred miles an hour.

I should have had a frankfurter, what these mixed up German gypsies have the gall to call *Americanos,* instead of attending an "American" Thanksgiving dinner at the Hotel de Paris' Michelin-approved Salle Empire Room. The turkey slices chewed like Vibram soles, the stuffing snapped, crackled and popped and the corn muffins would have been politely refused by starving children in Ethiopia. Never ask a French chef to cook American food.

The large, elegant banqueting hall with its colorful murals was dazzling, as were the white-jacketed waiters who frog-marched in like a parade of San Francisco gay rights activists. But this show of opulence made the contrast between ambience and food only starker. A French "country & western trio" tried to take our minds off the food by trashing Willie Nelson tunes.

If the Pilgrims had eaten and been entertained like this, they'd have turned around and sailed back to Europe.

* * *

Round about 3:30 every afternoon, they meet inside
the Green Dolphin, my lunchtime haunt. A handful of
English-speaking men of wealth. Some Americans. Some
English. At least one Canadian. Based on average Monaco
statistics, one is a penniless fraud, another a Carabinieri
informant. There is only one topic on the agenda: currency.
The key question is this: what is the value of the U.S.
dollar against the British pound, the Deutschmark, the
Japanese yen and the French franc?

None of the assembled ever know the precise answer
though the figures are available at the nearest bank, 35
within walking distance. But this unanswered question is
posed to commence a round of heated jawboning about
what is going to happen to currency fluctuations tomorrow, next week and next month.

This is the high point of the day for these elder expats,
who have little else to do or think about. By 4:30, after several rounds of cappucino, they are usually in agreement
about what will happen tomorrow. They get no further,
however, because what invariably happens tomorrow is the
opposite of today's consensus. So they have to start over
the next day.

Lyin' Leon is the high priest of the Green Dolphin's
currency wizards. He boasts of running 52 companies that
supposedly span the globe. And if it's true, the Dolphin
must be world headquarters, because that's where Leon
holds court six times a day, walking a beat between the
busy café and his Shangri-La apartment around the corner.
And if he sees you—bang!—you're nailed for another
30-minute discourse on the state of his worldly assets.

It's easy to tell when Lyin' Leon is telling a whopper.
His eyes bulge out of their sockets as he says, "I have three
Porsches back home," and he swings his head a full 90

degrees to the right, twisting his neck, as if to say, Here I go again…

7

Italy is only 20 minutes from Monaco. It's constantly in your face, calling out, "I'm-a-here—you-come-and-a-get-me!" And you want to reach out and grab it, because it appears, from a distance, to sum up what life is all about: impulse.

There's no question; you know intuitively when you cross the border from France into Italy, even if you miss the sign. It's a lot like going from the U.S. into Mexico. Suddenly, out of nowhere, the landscape glides from hillside villas with swimming pools to do-it-yourself vineyards. The driving turns anarchistic. Off go the seat belts. Down goes the accelerator. Beep goes the horn. It's every motorist for himself, insurance premiums be damned. You have, without a doubt, arrived in a highly-strung republic.

Italian-style driving is not for the weak of stomach. The timid better take a train. And everyone should take a bottle of Fernet-Branca. When you come to circles and mergers, you're automatically engaged in a contest that has nothing to do with the size of your car. It's called: who's got the biggest balls. The only way to drive in Italy is with your foot firmly planted on the gas pedal. Arm gestures are not only tolerated, they're encouraged. Swearing at slowpokes is a national sport and overtaking on hairpin turns is considered mundane.

The autoroute to Milano starts out rugged, mountainous, and takes you through about 150 tunnels, some lit, some not, all perilous. Overtaking inside tunnels is illegal, but this being Italy, who cares? You think you're going fast at 80 miles an hour until a Fiat whizzes around you, its driver cursing and honking at 120.

You hang a left at Genoa and leave the snow-capped Alps behind. The land becomes so flat and dull, you're excited to reach the outskirts of Milano even though it resembles suburban Warsaw.

But when you penetrate the cinderblock complexes and reach the city, you find volatile, bustling streets with a people louder and more expressive than the comparatively frigid French. This is a hot-blooded Latino mob and you can feel their intensity vibrating your bones. It seems like there is no order to anything. Then you realize it doesn't just *seem* that way, there *is* no order to anything.

The lights, the signs, the carnival of directions—they are all a charade to mix up tourists and amuse the natives. I made a wrong turn and found myself surrounded by a sea of people in Place Duomo, a pedestrian precinct and city epicenter. The harder I tried to rejoin road traffic, the more it eluded me. At three miles an hour, I desperately tried to cut a swath through the gaping, laughing and swearing hordes in search of a back street to make good my escape. But every road was blocked, to prevent other motorists from doing what I had achieved, and I became more deeply entrenched among the bemused Milanese.

A small blue Fiat marked "Polizia" pulled up alongside and, recalling accounts of on-the-spot "fines," I decided to take the upper hand.

"I hope *you* can explain what I'm doing here," I barked. Sufficiently intimidated by my dark glasses, and the New Jersey plates on my car, the olive-skinned officer performed a succession of frenetic arm gestures, less understandable than Italian, then disappeared into the throng. I made a U-turn and became as muddled as before. Enough. I braked the Jeep to a halt amongst the gawking mob and walked two blocks to my hotel.

The concierge laughed when I told him where I was parked.

"That's not the funny part," I said. "Here are the keys. It's *your* problem now!"

Parking is a free-for-all. You find cars parked on the sidewalk, in the park, stacked on top of each other—if there's a space, someone will fill it with a Fiat. Doesn't matter if you're *standing* in the space when they see it. If you aren't run-off by their blaring horn, they have no qualms about massaging your knees with their bumper. This is a touchy-feely people. They'll flip you the bird, drive you off the road, then invite you home for lasagna.

The green light at the street corner says *AVANTI*, but not even a chicken would cross an Italian road without looking every direction. Mopeds appear out of dark alleys, mounted by seemingly blindfolded drivers. Remember when you were a kid and you'd clip a stiff playing card onto your bicycle wheel so it would strike the spokes and create a clatter? That's how these motorized bikes sound, throw in screechy brakes and leaded exhaust fumes. They are the preferred mode of transport for commuters hoping to beat a maze of roads not built for late 20th century traffic. They are also favored by thieves to affect a quick getaway. These mobile muggers will relieve you of your continental-style handbag at 30 miles an hour, and by the time you know what hit you, the bandit is about a half-mile gone and fading fast. The general rule of thumb for Italy is this: if it's not bolted down, it's history.

Don't bother with the police unless you're insured and need to validate your claim. They'll tell you about a cousin in Hoboken or an uncle who worked for Al Capone, but they *won't* find your bag. They will, however, take careful note of what you lost so they'll know later exactly what their cut should be.

Milano is a shopping town, and everyone was feverish with total consumption. Along the fashionable Monte Napoleone consumers are mesmerized by the resplendent window displays of Gucci, Pucci and Wucci. Everything looks expensive at first glance—a million lire for this, two million for that—but once you've made the conversion… damn, it's still expensive! But you don't have to convert currency and be confused: the Italians *love* French francs and U.S. dollars; hell, they even prefer a *check* to Italian lire. The speed with which my assortment of currency vanished left me in no doubt that Christmas was approaching.

The Piazza del Duomo was chock-a-block with Santa Clauses and their cameramen. You are supposed to believe they will send you a photo two weeks after you pay them 20,000 spondulics to snap a vacant shutter release. The raunchy Santa my daughter raced to was mildly affectionate until he realized I wouldn't spring for a snap.

"He's not the real Santa anyway," said my daughter. "He doesn't speak English."

Yeah, even the dogs are mangy in Italy. Unlike the cared-for canines across the border, these poor pooches peer at you nervously, like they're used to getting their butts kicked; chronic constipation explains the absence of pavement poop.

8

You need to un-stress after Italy, shed a layer of anxiety and chill out your brain. The best way is an early evening walk through the narrow cobblestoned streets of the Rock. The old village bursts with character, mystique...with unusual odors (don't think for a minute you're going to get such eye-pleasing antiquity without ancient plumbing).

A quiet footpath around the back, overlooking the Med, leads down to the port, where an array of floating mansions are berthed, their handsome mahogany interiors freshly shined by boat monkeys. A stone jetty beckons you out to one of two lighthouses that punctuate the harbor entrance. Standing alone in the dark, you look across the port. Monaco is aglow beneath the dark, mysterious *Têt de Chien*. If the glow was green, and not golden, you would think of the Emerald City.

You look east, out through the night over the dark sea, beyond Cap Martin to the glittery lights of Italy in the distance—where it belongs—and the squiggles set in, from head to toe. You have found, while the sensation lasts, the center of your universe.

It is time for reflection, and a drink. And you've already discovered the one watering hole in Monaco that

can perpetuate the spiritual sensation you felt on the jetty:
Le Texan.

There is no pretension at Le Texan, on a Condamine
back street in the earthy port quarter. You step inside,
greeted by the piquant aroma of ham hock stewing in a
crock of beans, and this Tex-Mex saloon is immediately as
comfortable as your favorite pair of blue jeans. For a couple
of bucks you can linger over a bottle of Heineken, corn
chips and salsa at the long Alamo Bar and watch the diverse
cliques of Monaco mix it up: young international profes-
sionals here to transform the Principality from an upper-
crust retirement community to *the* financial center of
Europe; the Monegasque establishment; royalty; the neighborhood eccentrics, spies and celebrities. You see them all.

I saw an elegant madam dump her 20-grand mink coat
on a hat and coat stand near the door and disappear to a
table 'round the back. And then, as a corpulent, fruity
American expounded about Monaco's absence of crime,
the stand, laden with Italian leather and furs, toppled over
and mugged him.

Behind my cowhide-covered barstool, an English
couple engaged in a loud, profane spat. When these expat
Brits over-indulge in tequila, the Oxbridge accent mysteri-
ously disintegrates into a provincial, distinctly middle-class,
no, *lower* middle-class dialect, liberally sprinkled with *fook
yous*, *piss orfs* and *arsehole*.

As they heaped drunken abuse upon one another, Jaws
strode in. This is a big, bull-necked longshoreman-type,
the Brutus of Popeye cartoons, who everyone calls Jaws
because his only teeth are sharp canines, used for gnawing
nachos. Jaws sits at the bar and gulps pastis, a strong, cheap
licorice-flavored liquor, and smacks his tongue against the
roof of his mouth, sounding like a squirrel in heat. He

sometimes follows pretty waitresses into the communal washroom for an attempted grope, then washes his face and returns to his barstool, water dripping from his moist, grotesque mug.

On this night, Jaws brought in a nudie magazine and, *sans* reservation, plopped himself at a table adjacent the door and positioned his dirty book so that anyone coming or going would catch its bawdy cover full in the face.

"That dirty ol' Jaws," said Tony, scratching his head and making notes in the reservation book. "He's screwin' up mah floor-plan agin."

Everyone in the Principality comes equipped with a

story, and Tony's is as good as any. A black man, from
North Carolina, Tony hasn't been "home" since 1964
when he enlisted in the U.S. Army and got shipped to Germany. Set free after a two-year stint, he roamed Europe,
savored its fruit, picked up three languages doing nightclub
work in Germany, Holland and France before settling in
Rocquebrune, a stone's throw from Monaco. He hasn't
seen his mother or seven brothers and sisters in 25 years;
won't ever see his daddy again, ten years gone. Tony almost
went back twice, once after a sister was murdered ("It's a
good thing—I woulda killed a man"); another time, bags
packed, ticket in hand at an airport, Tony couldn't board
the plane. A little voice kept nagging him, "You can't go
home, Tony, you can't go home."

Now Tony works at Le Texan. And this is where he was
always meant to be.

"Who's that funny guy you's with the other night?"
Tony asked me.

"You mean Bob Bicker?"

"Bic-ker," Tony repeated. "Hmmmmm. Who he?
What's he *do*?

I didn't figure *Tony* as a Carabinieri informant, but this
being Monaco, you never know.

"Hot shot investment guy," I said. "Gives expensive
advice. Especially expensive to those who follow it. Why do
you ask?"

"He was in here last night acting peculiar. I just won-
dered who he is, that's all."

"Tony, this place is *full* of peculiar people. What did
Bicker do?"

"Well, it was weeeird. One minute he's sittin' inside,
next, he's out on the terrace, sitting' by hisself in the cold.
Then he's in again, out again, all the time with a real

strange look in his eye. And he hung 'round doin' this till closin' time, 'bout one-thirty in the mornin'."

Elsewhere, someone behaving like that might be suspected of casing the joint, or smoking one, but nobody cases or smokes joints in Monaco unless they want a cell with a sea view beneath the Jacques Cousteau Museum on the Rock.

"Bicker has an overblown ego," I explained. "And it got nailed a couple weeks ago when his wife walked. You know how it is, the bigger they are, the harder they fall."

Jaws finished gnawing at nachos and began to pace. Someone hummed the theme form Spielberg's classic as Jaws loomed heavily over Miss Katie, growling, again, about a date.

Miss Katie *is* Le Texan. A golden-haired, blue-eyed cactus flower in beat-up denim and cowboy boots, radiating raw spirit, Miss Katie runs the joint—and the quirky character cabaret—with a finesse unseen since Amanda Blake and her Long Branch Saloon graced our screens in "Gunsmoke."

Next night, Le Texan was buzzing with gossip about Bicker's beloved Lamborghini, totaled early that morning when Bicker's estranged, google-eyed wife drove into a wall at 120 miles an hour. She, miraculously, suffered only a broken thigh. But Bicker lost his prized auto *and* his pride when he rushed to her bedside, expecting these emotive circumstances to evolve into reconciliation. Not a chance. When his wife regained consciousness, she looked Bicker square in the face through honest, hung-over eyes and said, "I think you're repulsive."

This episode was related to me at Le Texan's Alamo Bar by Jake Miller, a tall, slim, balding, 60ish American expat. When you ask Miller what he does, he looks both ways, locks his eyeballs into yours, and whispers, "Problem-solver." It is, for him, an intense moment. You pry a tad further, mostly out of amusement, and he grows secretive, blasé, and murmurs haltingly about the State Department some years back. "Oh, the foreign service?" you ask. He affects a fast head nod to the affirmative, looks right and left, into his wine, and back into your eyes, and whispers, "Security, Eastern Europe," in one quick burst.

Jaws and Jake both are in love with Miss Katie, along with a dozen other Alamo Bar fixtures. And charismatic Kate knows how to treat each one like Marshal Matt Dillon.

9

If Monaco is a sunny place for shady people, Bavaria is the exact opposite: a shady place for sunny people. Bavarians are an obliging bunch, possessing big warm smiles and boundless energy. Their pitfall is the language. German doesn't just sound threatening, it *looks* threatening when you see it on road signs, menus and everyplace else.

Munich bustles with festive activity three days before Christmas. The lively old squares are crowded with booths selling wooden toys, hand-carved nativity scenes and colorful glass Christmas ornaments; the air full of heavenly aromas radiating from freshly-baked cookies, fruit dipped in hot chocolate sauce, and hot dog stands offering a choice of sizzling bratwurst, knockwurst, this-wurst, that-wurst and, of course, the *americano*. Men huddle around a schnapps stall, throwing back shots to warm their insides. Nobody minds a light drizzle.

The large, jolly restaurants are a maze of rooms that keep going and don't stop. Winding up some stairs, around the back, each nook and cranny with a different menu, if serviced by the same kitchen. The wooden Alpine tables are packed with laughing Bavarians, eating roast suckling pig or wienerschnitzel, everything *mid* sauerkraut, and drinking, from large steins, the finest beer in the world

After a full day and night of this we headed south, magnificent snow-covered mountains looming before us, until we were consumed by them, the Bavarian Alps, and then, with a friendly wave, across the quiet country border into Austria, Germany's poor little brother.

Our driver hadn't heard heard of Achenkirch, our holiday destination, and this was not a good sign, especially since he had attended school nearby. My brother Michael made all the arrangements six months earlier, site unseen, for this Christmas family rendezvous in the Tyrol. It did look magical in the brochure: lakeside setting, majestic peaks, quaint town.

At first glance, Achenkirch was unimpressive as we cruised past several chateaus and on into the center. The most striking thing about the town was there wasn't any. Just our sprawling Posthotel, a church and a modern Spar *supermarkt* across the street. At second glance, Achenkirch remained unimpressive. Where were the charming cobblestoned streets with cutesy shops and frescoed walls?

I found my brother looking sheepish inside the lobby; he'd arrived 20 minutes earlier from London. Mike shrugged, pleaded hunger and raced off to find frankfurters and sauerkraut.

A minor expedition was necessary to reach my room: an elevator in the main building to the first floor, a walk down a long corridor connecting the old complex with the new annex, a second elevator to the third floor. It wasn't worth the trip. You couldn't swing a cat in my room; the bath towels were the sort you use for dish-drying—and there wasn't enough wattage in the lightbulbs to read a book. I went back down to protest.

"Don't worry about the room," said the smiling proprietor in earnest (we were captive guests). "You'll be outdoors most of the time."

So I went outside to see what I'd be doing and nearly froze my butt off. There was one main road and I walked it half-a-mile. Nobody seemed to *stop* in Achenkirch; it is a drive-through town, and I had to dive for cover in the slush every time a car came barreling through.

I walked back to the hotel and inquired at the desk about local transportation for leaving town. There wasn't any. Then I went to find my brother. He must have sensed I was going to strangle him as he filled his face with potato dumplings, because he threw up his arms and said, "It's Christmas! At least we're together!"

Together? His two little girls were already fencing with frankfurters and stockpiling sauerkraut for an imminent escalation.

I'd sworn off drink for the holiday, but quickly deduced I'd better have a beer. I hit the bar, started drinking beer with Mike, and didn't stop. It took the barkeep, a real craftsman, a few minutes to pour each draft from the tap—let it settle, add a little more, et cetera. So we started ordering two, then three beers at a time—got an assembly line going so there were always a couple of beers on the bar waiting to be drunk. It took about six of these babies before I began to appreciate the Tyrol.

A large buffet was laid out: thin slices of smoked duck, smoked goose with raspberry sauce, smoked ham, wild mushroom casserole, onion pie, lentil soup, four kinds of salad, three kinds of home-baked bread—and that was just the first course.

We ate. And drank more beer. The kids rose from the table and raced with laughter through the maze of eating areas, bars and nooks and crannies. That was the beauty of this place: you could turn them loose and nobody cared; the staff smiled cheery smiles and constantly asked if everything was all right. "Fine, fine. Give us another six beers." And so on into the night.

Blissfully bongoed around midnight, Mike and I took a stroll through the village. The air was crisp and the surrounding snowy mountains shone bluish-white beneath a bright moon.

We trudged through snow and slush until we arrived at a *gasthaus*, about a mile away, and ordered a couple large steins of beer, to fortify us for the slog back.

Later I staggered around the sprawling hotel, an early morning exploration to master its amenities while everyone slept. A sign in the basement that said "Teestube Chamber" stumped me. I peeked inside: small purple bathtubs with odd-looking valves and nozzles, an embalmer's paradise!

So much for the amenities.

Come sunrise, Christmas Eve, we took a sleigh ride. My wife got pelted on the cheek when the sleigh driver cracked back his whip: old-fashioned whiplash. Back home you would sue for a million bucks worth of punitive damage, but all you can do here is grab a handful of ice and laugh.

That night we observed a traditional Christmas Eve inside the hotel. Guests and staff, dressed in Sunday best, assembled inside the main lounge, a large comfortable room furnished with overstuffed couches, armchairs and coffee tables. Young children sang festive carols, and a candle-lit mass was delivered in German. Then the genuine fir tree was lighted with real candles and St. Nicholas arrived with a sackful of presents for the children. My daughter got a Donald Duck comic book, in German. We sipped mugs of *gluden*, hot mulled wine, and later, as I prepared for bed near midnight, the church bells chimed to herald the arrival of Christmas, and carolers outside the hotel sang "Silent Night" as I drifted into a dream.

The day after Christmas I was struck by a fever, a virulent strain of flu making the rounds through northern Europe. I became delirious that night, awakening drenched in sweat, needing water, then suffering cold chills as I crept back to bed. I repeated my thirst-quenching mission throughout the cursed night—the worst in my life—each time stumbling over a suitcase or stubbing a toe. I felt like I was going to die.

A doctor arrived the next day, an old-world, hotel-calling Tyrolean physician, husky and gray, wearing an Alpine hat. He spoke German to himself as he examined my aching person.

"*Der grippe*," he finally diagnosed, and he reached deep into his brown leather bag for a dose of strong antibiotics.

My only escape from misery was a British satellite TV channel that broadcast reruns of "I Dream of Jeannie" and "The Ghost and Mrs. Muir." After day three of this torment I reached my lowest ebb, and swore at myself for leaving the comforts of New Jersey. I pined for my spacious bedroom and high-pressure shower, for NyQuil, for my mother-in-law's barley soup.

Achenkirch was to blame for the malady, for confining me without mercy. I had let down my defenses to the village and it devoured my spirit. And sure enough, *der grippe* only released its grasp when I rolled free of the Tyrol, toward Munich *flugenhof*.

10

Ma Kelly laid into Jaws right after Christmas, told him to stay the hell out of her saloon. Forty years ago this feisty lady was Grace Kelly's roommate at New York's Barbizon, where acting students were roomed alphabetically. They became close friends and both wound up in Monaco, Grace, as princess, and Kelly, as wife to the conductor of Monaco's symphony orchestra. Now Ma Kelly, Miss Katie's mom, is matriarch at Le Texan.

Kelly's cadre of chums includes the Dick Sisters, a pair of jet-set homos who breeze into the Principality for a spot of high society shit-stirring, then steal off to Switzerland until the heat dies down. The duo's senior fruit, Dickie, was trained as a court jester and says things like, "I knew Gucci when he used to repair my shoes," and "I'm the one who taught Robert Carrier how to cook." His notoriety along the Riviera stems from the time he spiked a birthday cake with LSD at a high society bash. Lady Somebody-or-other almost killed herself driving home to Cap Ferrat in reverse.

Jake Miller was conspicuous in his absence from the Alamo Bar. All Tony would say about the incident was, "Man, he's a *weeirrd* dude." But I found out what had happened.

Miller, convinced Cupid had discharged an arrow on New Year's Eve, could no longer contain his lust for Miss Kate. He hugged her tight, wouldn't let go, and Tony had to pry him loose.

Without Jaws and the spook, Le Texan is a little less like the bar in *Star Wars,* but not much less, especially with Bicker around.

When Randy Newman wrote "Small People," he was thinking of Bob Bicker. Walking with him one night toward Le Texan, this smug little guy sneezed and inadvertently blew a fart so enormous, it propelled him six-feet forward.

Bicker likes expensive ornaments. He sports a top-of-the-line gold and diamond-studded Rolex, carries a crocodile attache case and chain smokes with a gold Dunhill lighter. Throw in his bouffant hair-do, shi-shi cigarette holder and effeminate gestures, and you've got the know-it-all caterpillar in *Alice in Wonderland.*

Bicker and I got round to discussing the meaning of life over half-a-dozen bottles of mood enhancer at Le Texan's Alamo Bar.

"It all comes down to one thing," said Bicker. "Getting laid."

And I gather this is on his mind since he *isn't.*

"Procreation," he continued. "That's the bottom line."

"Maybe," I offered, "it's because when you die your spirit joins your offspring whose physical composition is genetically derived from you." I was nudging. Bicker has no children, wants none and has been estranged from his parents for a decade.

"I don't buy it," said Bicker, with typical finality. "When you die, you're done."

The smoke from his burning cigarette curled up into my nostrils and mouth, and I stood there choking, coughing, spluttering, as he lit another.

Miss Katie overheard our metaphysical mumblings and contributed an interest in psychic healers and spiritual guides, saying that she visits a tarot card reader and runs Le Texan on positive energy, juggling overlapped reservations with the right vibes. It's down to Tony, a natural skeptic, to keep everything in perspective with a well-placed "don't give me that shit." The chemistry between them works better than Huntley-Brinkley.

Roberto sauntered in, hands on his hips, smiling and looking around the joint. Squat, olive-skinned and from Milano, Roberto dresses in blue denim from neck to ankle and wears face cream in his curly black locks to give it a "just washed" lustre.

His nightly circuit in pursuit of *verge du jour*, virgin of the day, takes him to Café de Paris, the piano bar at Loews Hotel, Le Texan and finally to Jimmy'z Discotech. He stalks American teenage girls, offering to be their guide around Monaco "no strings attached." Near the end of a late supper, he croons, "Are we going to bed?" If the answer is *no*, he argues the point; if it's still no, he gets up without a word and disappears, leaving her with the tab.

Roberto hangs out with Lorenzo; sometimes they do the circuit together. Lorenzo struts the floor at Le Texan like Mussolini, scowling at the men and checking out the women. If their looks don't please him, he marches out.

Often, Roberto operates as Lorenzo's advance man, looking for talent and, if found, keeps them charmed till Lorenzo arrives for an inspection.

On this evening, Roberto ground to a halt near four young American girls standing at the Alamo Bar, margaritas lined up in front of them. His expression said he couldn't believe his luck and I watched him search for an angle, the right position, eyes alert, never departing his prey. He elbowed a space, wedged in next to them, dipped into their basket of cornchips, and munched, awaiting an opportunity to deliver his favorite opener: "I can see deep into your eyes. You are a lonely woman. And I'm a lonely man. Let's spend some time together."

You could tell he wanted to dash to a telephone—"come quick, Lorenzo, two for you and two for me!"—but he dared not leave his spot for a second because he observed Shorty dining at a table nearby. And it was just a matter of time before Shorty would sneak over to the girls with promises of a date with Prince Albert.

11

The way Carabinieri Control stakes out Monaco's train station, you'd think they were expecting Saddam Hussein. If someone rolls in to whom they take an arbitrary dislike—wrong clothes, scuffed shoes, no Vuitton luggage—they conduct an open-air interrogation. I saw an owlish nerd carrying a duffel bag, fresh off a train, no doubt thinking he'd take in the sights, maybe toss some dice...no way, José. The poor sucker got about 20 yards before they nabbed him on the forecourt, scrutinized his ID and, in an attempt to be democratic, held a vote amongst themselves whether to release or bounce him. The assembled bystanders wanted blood. I rooted for the nerd, and for one mad moment considered throwing down a roll of toilet paper from my writing hideaway in Le Siecle.

The nerd lost the election, and he was invited to stow his cheapo bag in the trunk of a police car, then whisked to the Italian border, kicked in the butt and advised to visit Milano instead.

The *National Enquirer* had reported that Monte Carlo is rampant with junkies, so Carabinieri Control was cracking down on anyone looking like an *Enquirer* reporter.

* * *

The Hotel Le Siecle's proprietor, Monsieur Molass, is not a professional hotelier, but an engineer who got into the business by accident. Every Thursday night his lobby plays venue to what I at first thought was the Monegasque National Council: a cluster of graying, distinguished gentlemen, hemming and hawing, occasionally snoring. It was, I discovered, the Dutch Millionaires of Monaco club, a holdover from the previous ownership.

Molass bought the 39-room hotel from a Dutchman, and was sorry almost immediately. Local merchants appeared on his doorstep and presented hefty bills supposedly left unpaid by the previous owner. Molass denied liability, but the bailiff sided every time with Monegasque creditors. The legal paperwork alone gave him five-day migraines.

Still optimistic, Molass installed a piano near the bar, and, emulating an American tradition, launched a happy hour. It was very happy indeed, until the Carabinieri marched in and ended the fun. No entertainment license. You would think bureaucracy in a sovereign state smaller than Central Park would not be so demanding. A year later, Molass was still completing forms in quintuplicate.

There are others, like the Rigatonis, builders friendly to the palace, who find the system, shall we say, *less* demanding. Their plans for razing quaint four-story apartment buildings with shuttered windows and wrought-iron balconies to make way for concrete and glass multistory eyesores seem to breeze right through.

With gross redevelopment underway, the Monegasques are shifted out of Condamine and into Funnyville, the new sinking suburbs behind the Rock. This is supposed to create a clear field for the multimillionaires being wooed from Hong Kong.

* * *

Before coming to Monaco, I applied for a 12-month French visa, the first step toward a Monaco residency permit, the much-coveted *carte de sejour*.

First, you have to complete a two-sided orange form, in French, seven times, each of which requires a photograph. Next, you have to get a letter from your bank manager confirming your ability to support yourself for the duration of your stay in France (they don't want you stealing a job from a Frenchman). This has to be translated into French. Next, a medical examination to establish your good health, conducted by one of *their* approved physicians for $150. This has to be translated into French. Next, a letter from your local police chief, affirming your good behavior. This has to be translated into French. Next, a letter from a lawyer, confirming that you have never gone bankrupt. This has to be witnessed and stamped by a notary public, and, yes, translated into French.

If you pass muster and Paris gives the green light, you graduate to step two. You must visit Carabinieri Control within two weeks of your arrival in Monaco. They make arrangements for *The Interview*, at which your intentions and finances are scrutinized by the chief of the *Bureau d'Etranger*. If you pass this, they grant you a *"temporaire" carte de sejour*, good for one year. After three of these, you are promoted to *"ordinaire"* status, good for three years. After three of these, and three more interviews, you finally qualify for a *carte de privilege*, good for ten years. (Monegasque nationality is almost impossible to obtain, granted only by the Sovereign.)

When your *carte* expires, you are told to bring your Monegasque electricity and telephone bills to the renewal

interview. They determine from these how much of the
year you have spent in the Principality, and if they conclude
you have spent less than six months, your residency status
is terminated. For the key word here is "spent." They want
residents who are going to *spend money*.

Step three. You have passed steps one and two. Now it's
time to cough up. You brought over a car? Boom. As fast
as they fit you with prestigious Monegasque plates, you are
handed a tax bill for one-third your vehicle's value. Oh,
plus one-third what you paid to ship it over, including
insurance. Boom. You've got two weeks to fit your head-
lights with yellow lamps and make other adjustments to
your car. Then you may be asked to "host" an event. One
lady got stuck with a bill for five grand after agreeing to
"host" a dinner for a visiting Hungarian soccer team.

I never got beyond step one. The French Consulate cannot permit the sovereignty of France to be insulted by poor
grammar so, unhappy with my translation, they returned
the whole package, unprocessed, and thereby saved me
from steps two and three.

I came to Monaco anyway, unstamped and unregulated
into the system. My Jeep, with its New Jersey plates, is in
a kind of automobile no-man's-land, accountable to no
authority, and I'm about the same. I *do* have to step out of
France every 90 days. But this merely means crossing the
border into Ventimglia, crossing back, and getting my passport pounded.

12

Recuping with flu and zapped with lag, Winston flew in from Chicago for a visit. He, the former Time Inc. phraseologist who could summarize *War and Peace* in 40 lines, then psychoanalyze each character just for kicks.

"That's a three-look view," said Winston, admiring the old town of Villefranche as we chugged toward Monaco from Nice, he absorbing everything at breakneck speed, opening his spirit to the space.

It seemed like a good idea to take him to Le Texan straight away to smooth out the rough edges. Barry Schwartz was there. The recluse that he is, even Barry the Lamster found Le Texan. He's a world renowned investment guru, a mega-millionaire who rarely ventures from his Monte Carlo sanctuary. Hollywood would cast him as a flasher in his old overcoat and leering smile, and Tony, knowing no better, sat him at Jaw's old place near the door. That's where I found him, peering at me through the picture window, stabbing at enchiladas.

Barry is tough on new people, assuming they're part of the Big Brother-IRS-Trilateral Commission conspiracy until proven innocent. Thus he approached Winston with caution at the Alamo Bar.

"What's your sign?" he sneered, bringing his face so close to Winston's that their noses almost touched.

"My sign?" Winston had already been briefed on Le Texan, but Barry the Lamster is something else.

"When were you born?" Barry barked impatiently. Time is money to Barry; precisely $2600 an hour. He is hard of hearing, so he cupped a hand over his right ear and maneuvered it an inch from Winston's lips.

"Oh, uhhh, Capricorn."

Barry nodded, poker-faced.

I told Barry that Winston had arrived a few hours earlier from the States.

"I'd rather be a beggar in Europe than a millionaire in America," sniffed Barry. Then he leaned forward and whispered in my ear. "Who is the tall, balding American sitting behind me near the window?"

"You mean Jake Miller, superspook?"

"I thought so!" snapped Barry.

I waited out a minute of silence. You could *hear* the little cogs inside Barry's brain, clicking feverishly.

"What makes you ask?" I finally said.

"I've heard this guy Miller is investigating me!"

"Barry," I said, "you think *everybody* is investigating you. What makes Miller so special?"

"Bob Bicker told me. Says Miller's diggin' up dirt on me for *The Times* of London."

"Barry," I said, "Miller couldn't find a snatch in a whorehouse. Shall we call him over to talk about it?"

"No, no, no!" said Barry, shifting nervously.

Behind him, Miller rose and took position at the bar. He was craning his long neck, like a giraffe, trying to hone in on our conversation. I looked up.

"Hi, Jake, how ya doin'?"

"Oh, yes, fine," he said quickly, glancing up, down, sideways, finally resting his furtive eyes on the bar.

This was too much for Barry. Socializing is harder work for him than analyzing stock market trends, and his quota for the month was over after an hour at Le Texan. He dumped his drink, flashed a leer and disappeared down a Condamine back street to elude surveillance, pockets bulging with gold Kruggerands and six different passports.

Prince Albert, decked out in a cowboy shirt and blue jeans, was throwing back slammers with the boys while his 80 year-old uncle, Prince Louis de Polignac, held court with strolling mariachis.

Albert hangs out at Le Texan. His bodyguards, un-equipped with dark glasses and wires sticking out their ears, hang there too, a couple of ordinary Pierres in sports dress. And then there's Shorty, always Shorty, rounding up girls too young for Roman Polanski. Some folks call Shorty "the colonel," but when you say "that little wimp," everyone knows who you mean.

Miss Katie popped up from the Prince's table with a question for me. I was standing at the bar with Winston, feeding his fever and jet lag with Heineken.

"Albert wants to know about *that* guy," said Katie, pointing at Jake Miller down the bar.

Whoa, what happened to Carabinieri Control?

"Miller's a private dick," I said. "With emphasis on *dick*. And he seems to be getting popular."

"But what does he do?" asked Katie.

"Missing dog inquiries. Big business in that 'round here."

Tony overheard my conversation, like he overhears everything, and tried to make conversation with the disen-gaging dick as he poured him another glass of *rouge*.

"So," says Tony, "I hear you're some kinda dogcatcher or somethin'?"

Miller gagged.

Winston surveyed the whole scene, took it all in…the peg-legged Italian cuddling up to a wooden bust of General Custer, Jake Miller, superspook, glancing furtively at every-one, Miss Katie in her skin-tight blue jeans, Prince Albert, Uncle Louis, Colonel Shorty and the babes, Hamtown

Stubbs, a real Irish aristocrat (bombed, again), and Crazy George... Winston studied the whole bizarre scene, then turned to me and said, "It's kind of like the 'Aspen Cool,' but better. This is the 'Monaco Cool'."

Monaco Cool. Only four hours in town, the master phraseologist from the American heartland had defined the hitherto undefinable. Monaco Cool.

Crazy George, standing next to us, surveyed the scene, too, and added, less profoundly, "I've got to find something to schtoink."

"My God," he told Winston, eyes gleaming, "you have to come back in the summer and go to the beach, see those topless broads. What blows my mind is watching them *undress* on the beach. I had to stay in the water for half-an-hour!"

Jake Miller was now watching us intently, though he'd swing his narrow head around whenever we'd return the gaze.

"Who's he?" asked Crazy George.

"A spouse spy," I said. "He thinks you're involved in one of his matrimonial disputes and has been following you around for a week."

"Nah," said George. He paused a moment and snuck a peek down the bar at Miller, who caught George's eye and swung his head 500 miles an hour in the opposite direction. "Really?"

"Yep. When you leave here tonight, he'll be 20 steps behind. Look out your window at three in the morning. He'll be there, on the sidewalk looking up."

Crazy George turned again and faced Miller, four stools down the bar. "Is that a pickle in your pocket or are you just happy to see me?" said George.

Miller, now and forever the Pickleman, looked right, left, up and down, ran an extended forefinger from his chin over his lips past his nose, then beat a hasty exit out the door, in cold pursuit, no doubt, of Barry the Lamster. And later, perhaps, to a secret mission in his bathtub.

13

"I think I could get used to La-La land real easy," said Winston. We were lounging outside the Café de Paris, sipping frothy cappucino and soaking up rays in early February.

That is the essence of Monaco Cool: sitting, sipping, soaking and watching. Especially if these strenuous activities are performed after a workout, sauna, jacuzzi and rubdown at Loews health spa overlooking the sea. This sets you up for the day. In fact, why leave? You can stay the whole morning and afternoon for a measley 11 francs, the price of a cappucino. You can peruse the English newspapers; read a book, write one, and all the while grow a George Hamilton suntan on your face.

People-watchers have a field day: Ringo Starr will walk by in shorts; at another table you'll see Karl Lagerfeld, who designs Princess Caroline's clothes and is whispered to wear them before she does. Assorted billionaires and monarchs-in-exile parade by, sporting jewels they dare not exhibit elsewhere, and sometimes take them into Wurtz, the world's most exclusive pawn shop. Wurtz is a depot for precious family heirlooms, and it's probably no accident that it sits adjacent to the Grand Casino.

Have you ever seen a Rolls Royce-Ferrari-Lamborghini

traffic jam? You will outside the Café de Paris. And you might even see Elvis.

I asked Winston if Monaco Cool, as he conceived it, had a deeper meaning.

"Part of it is the bubble, once removed from reality. But state of mind is the most important element."

"Go on," I prodded.

"Feeling like you own the place. Monaco Cool is freedom."

"Are you nuts? What about all these cameras and carbinieris tracking every movement?"

"Ah, you've got it upside down," said Winston. "No one needs a defensive guard in Monaco *because* of the policing. Everyone checks their attitude at the border. Everyone's free to be friendly."

And he's right, old Winston, the police *salute* when you approach to ask directions. Not like state troopers back home, unbuttoning their holsters.

Monaco Cool is an exercise in the art of relaxation, stress-neutralizing, compounded with the Frenchman's appreciation for good food, fine wine and zest for the quality of life—and a dash of Italian anarchy and madness. Most of all, Monaco Cool is the character *you* inject into the multinational community.

"Monaco Cool," said Winston, "is Coca-Cola served in glass bottles instead of aluminum cans."

Le Texan is the hub of Monaco Cool, combining the ambience of an intercultural "Cheers" with a cast out of *One Flew Over the Cuckoo's Nest*. Winston and I sauntered into our favorite saloon and immediately, simultaneously, recognized Monaco Cool personified: Crazy George, clad in plaid shirt, sneakers, dirty white socks and his shit-eating grin, legs crossed and sprawled out like he's sitting in his own kitchen, sucking on a spoon.

Crazy George. Commodity trader by day, party animal at night, and after two hours' sleep, professor of statistics at Monaco's new university in Funnyville. He is *not* a millionaire, but has been able to wangle membership in The Club anyway, as part of the 15 percent not unemployed. And those 15 percent are the happiest people in Monaco—the Monaco Coolest.

Crazy George was sitting with the Swede, another child of Monaco Cool. The Swede is an assistant manager at Café de Paris—for which he earns a meager salary—but this being Monaco, he enjoys a jet-setting lifestyle, without the jets. Le Texan is the launching pad from which the Swede and Crazy George hit the Principality's exclusive nightspots.

They took Winston and me for a spin at high speed around the Grand Prix circuit and screeched to a halt in front of Jimmy'z. In his Ray-Ban Wayfarers, the Swede cut a swath through the throng of would-be nightclubbers who, for one reason or another, did not rank admission to the swanky club. The thing to say is that there's a bottle with your name on it inside, your "investment," but who knows that except the Monaco Cool? Winston and I followed behind Crazy George, taking notes.

The door swung open and Frankie, the manager, greeted the Swede with a warm smile and a kiss on each cheek. We trailed behind, into the meat market. At Jimmy'z there is no ground meat, no fatty chops, certainly no offal. Only prime rib and filet mignon.

The Swede had arranged a little treat for himself and Crazy George: four Swedish au-pairs who trained in from Nice. George, expecting a double-schtoink, sprang for two bottles of Taittinger at 175 bucks a pop. The girls gaily threw back the bubbly, then slipped off into the night with four dark Italians.

Prince Albert was bopping around the dance floor, and Shorty, never far away, was taking numbers from blonds and trying to choreograph the Prince toward his next dance partner.

Roberto hovered nearby, hoping to pick up royal rejects, telling one, "I'm rich, I'm handsome and all the girls want me."

In a far corner, the Rah-Rah Girls, a pair of New England quidnuncs, virgins, 35-ish, were clacking mental notes about who was cheating whom—tomorrow's scuttlebutt. Winston bought a round of drinks—about five—and got a bill for 150 bucks. It didn't phase him for a second because he had Mexican Ana, one of Miss Katie's girls, alone at the bar, and 20 minutes of gazing into Ana's big brown eyes, he said, was a bargain at twice the price.

14

The two worst influences on my liver arrived in town, unbeknownst to each other, but nonetheless on board the same Nice-bound airliner from London: my brother Mike, who radiates "booze binge" at the sight of me; and Roddy, a Fleet Street "diarist," a quaint English newspaper euphemism for gossip columnist. In the best tradition of Britain's tabloid reporters, Roddy never suffers hangover because he wakes up woofled and starts right in again.

Also on board: two terrorists, my nieces, the frankfurter fencers from the Tyrol. We dumped them as fast as possible at the elegant Hotel Hermitage, where they proceeded to renovate the suite a la Rod Stewart, and took position in the open-air at Café de Paris. We meant to have cappucino—it was only teatime—but bottles of Heineken arrived instead, and kept arriving at a rapid pace as the sun dipped slowly behind the *Tet de Chien*. A chilly dusk drove us down to the piano bar at Loews, where a major wetting down was in progress among participants of an International Television Festival. There is always something like this going on in the neighborhood. This was the catchphrase Roddy quickly devised for Monaco. The Neighborhood.

Roddy was in town at my invitation to pen his Sunday

"diary" from The Neighborhood. The deadline he faced was only 36 hours away, and he still had no inkling what his lead story might be.

"Something always turns up," he said whimsically, and ordered another round of Heineken.

Too many beers later, we roared out of Monte Carlo's marble, glass and stereoed parking lot and continued our binge at Hotel Le Siecle. That's where we moved into pastis, and Roddy threw back a half-dozen glasses of the potent libation while the Dutch Millionaires Club held council nearby.

We set off for Le Texan in search of nachos, gossip and more cactus juice. Surprise! The terrorists lay in wait, including my own little girl, their latest recruit. That meant their mommies were there, too. Tony tried to warn me of the ambush when I staggered in, but I was too slow on the draw, my mental reflexes neutered by beer and pastis. The onslaught was awesome. As I sat down, a tortilla chip loaded with guacamole whizzed past my head, and the look in my wife's eyes was sharper than a caseful of sushi knives. There was only one thing to do: order tequila.

Straight tequila is a lot like a woman's breasts. One is not enough; three, too many. But they kept coming, one after the other, in quick succession as we practiced the ritual again and again. A few specks of salt on the tongue, a shot of tequila drained, a slice of lemon sucked dry. As we drank, the terrorists pulled off minor acts of sabotage, like tripping a waitress, creating works of abstract art with salsa and sour cream and flinging hot chilies at anyone who dared throw a disapproving glance.

At some point, Miss Katie's brother, Mike, walked past. Mike is Prince Albert's best buddy and knows all the celebs by proxy.

"I've got some great news!" he announced. "Isaac and Maureen are getting married!" He was talking about Isaac Tigrett, cofounder of the Hard Rock Cafe, and Maureen Starkey, ex-wife of Ringo Starr. This was especially great news for Roddy, whose lead story for Sunday—"Mrs. Ringo is Ringing off at Last"—arrived on a wooden platter, amid yet another round of tequila.

The wives left in disgust, terrorists in tow, and we moved our binge to the Alamo Bar, where even Crazy George wanted nothing to do with us.

My brother Mike and I launched into each other animatedly as Roddy smiled his gossip columnist's smarmy English smile and missed nothing, though totally soused, which for him was business as usual.

"Tony!" I shouted. "I'll give you 500 francs to come 'round here and beat the shit out of my brother!"

Miss Katie interceded with another round of tequila, on-the-house. That's the Le Texan philosophy: if something's wrong, throw tequila at it.

Mike called me a name, then asked how *that* grabbed me.

"I think *you* should *grab* that cactus over there," I told him, pointing at the Alamo Bar mascot, a phallic and gonad-shaped cactus, "and shove it up your ass!"

"I'd be happy to grab it," said Mike, "but I think I'll shove it up *your* ass!"

"Oh," Roddy chirped in, with his English capricious air, "Is that a Texan custom?"

I'd had enough, and was ready to lay down my glass. But Miss Katie poured another complimentary refill. I'd *never* get out of there.

"What's the answer to it all?" I asked Roddy, rhetorically.

"Forty-two," he replied, without a moment's hesitation.

"Forty-two what?"

"Just forty-two."

When I awoke, the next morning, I was sorry I did. My head pounded, my tongue was fuzzy and thick and most of my brain remained switched off throughout the day in an attempt to unpickle itself. My mouth tried desperately to make coherent conversation, but my mind refused to cooperate, and I'd be stuck in mid-sentence—an *easy* sentence—groping for an elusive word or phrase.

Mike, too, was whacked out and, smarter than me, didn't even try to rouse himself. Roddy didn't feel a thing. His brain plays games when he *doesn't* drink.

I had to get up when I heard my wife's commotion in the kitchen, where the combo washer-dryer was spinning half-heartedly, sputtering strange sounds and discharging gallons of water onto the floor.

The plumber gave a quick inspection, then charged 250 francs to say we needed a washing machine "specialist."

A specialist arrived the next day, pulled the machine from beneath the sink, then shook his head solemnly.

"I'm sorry," he whispered.

Five months after buying it from the former tenant as part of the *reprise*, my washer-dryer had OD'd on detergent. The specialist pointed to a small label at the rear of the machine, suggesting this was the reason for its untimely demise. The label said: "Made in Italy."

I knew a replacement would be expensive, but I had to reach for more Bufferin when Monsieur Baldo, the specialist's boss, announced a price three times what a washing machine twice its load capacity would cost at Sears.

15

Bills of all kinds were arriving. Utility statements from back home, sent by boat, payment long overdue and disconnection imminent; an indecipherable telephone bill in French, *un*-itemized, of course, its astronomical demand courtesy of the Philippine babysitter.

I went to my office at Hotel Le Siecle, and *their* bill awaited me. "Fuck this!" I yelled up to the *Tet de Chien*. "I'm going to Paris!" Perfect, because you need an attitude for Paris.

It took only a few hours to make bookings, grab a helicopter, a shuttle and, swish, we were there, in the New York City of France. If the French were smiling at Americans in Paris, then surely, it wouldn't be long before pigs take flight.

The taxi driver, all Gallic grunts, didn't smile, but he *did* take the most direct route from Orly to the *1st arrondissement* and did not protest our noisy family game of "Who Can Spot the Eiffel Tower First?"

The expressionless bellhop led the way to our room on the third floor of the Intercontinental. 'Round a corner, quick left, long corridor, left again past the stairs, right, left, right... I tried to memorize the route, but should have brought a *baguette* and left a trail of crumbs. Switched on the TV set: "I Dream of Jeannie"... again... this time in German; part of the plan to unify Europe—unify it with sixties, American culture.

We dumped our bags and tried to find the elevator. A number of twists and turns later, we found ourselves standing outside our room. The problem with hotels like the Intercontinental is that it takes 10 minutes to get outside, and that's only if you don't get lost or side-tracked by a bar.

The choice of a place to eat was clear, even if we didn't have a reservation.

"Rue Marbeuf," I instructed the cabbie.

"Andre?" he asked.

"*Oui, Monsieur.*"

"*C'est bon,*" he grunted his approval, and *smiled.*

The Parisian cuisine outranks just about anything served along the Cote d'Azur, including seafood. And at *Chez Andre* you can feast on green beans alone. There are two evening shifts. The first, commencing at 7pm, is comprised exclusively of Americans. We are renowned in France for eating early and eating fast, and we are expected to vacate our tables at 8:30 so the serious, French shift can begin, and this one continues till midnight.

After dinner, the best spot from which to observe the Eiffel Tower is Trocadero, a bustling intersection with a vibrant open-air café on every corner. The ideal vantage point is Café du Trocadero. You can sit over a costly cappucino and mull over Eiffel's *pièce de spectacle*. A century ago, most of Paris was up in arms over Eiffel's "1,050-foot lightning rod." But these same folks didn't like Van Gogh either.

Next, the Champs Elysees, its 15 cinemas playing 30 year-old Jerry Lewis movies to packed houses. My wife and little girl retired for a dose of mass hypnosis, and I retreated to the Hemingway Bar at the rear end of The Ritz, Paris's swankiest hotel. To reach the bar from the front entrance on Place Vendome you have to run the Ritz Gauntlet. This is a narrow red-carpeted hall lined on each side with a glass showcase, displaying for a hundred yards the most beautiful material possessions in the world, all beckoning your American Express Card. I tried to keep my eyes fixed straight ahead, like a horse wearing clappers, and was okay...until I caught a glimpse of a Paris street scene in oil by Edouard Cortes. This stumped me; I'm a sucker for warmly-lit cafés contrasted with a rainy dusk. Then the $300 shoes. The kind that call out to your feet on a wavelength only feet can hear. "Hey, you two, come back. You need me!" I walked faster, heart pounding, trying to beat the damn gauntlet. Mont Blanc pens, Cartier watches, Kenzo ties...I made it! Or did I? Suddenly I hungered for a crocodile belt.

The Hemingway Bar is a cozy den where Ernie, in his ritzy years, had a drink and probably reminisced about his poorer, happier years in Montparnasse. On the bar is a bronze bust of old Hem looking smug.

For the full experience, I ordered the Hemingway Cocktail, a concoction of orange juice, whiskey and Drambouie, served in a martini glass with a crushed ice and a maraschino cherry at the end of a toothpick. It wasn't bad. But it wasn't worth 13 bucks. Especially after the bartender told me it wasn't Hem's drink at all; he favored a dry martini.

I wandered up Rue de la Paix to Place L'Opera. They say if you sit outside the Café de la Paix long enough, you'll see half the people you know. Probably the half you tried to forget about. I stood a safe distance away, watching the people watchers. Then I cut into Harry's Bar and ordered a dry martini. A whole brigade of middle-aged Japs trooped into Harry's, took a long look 'round the joint and marched back out. I guess Harry's was on their shopping list, too, along with the Mona Lisa and half the city's real estate. Their idea of a memento from France is a Cezanne or a Renoir, plus a carton of Hermes scarves.

Next morning I took my daughter to a toy store on St. Honore and offered *her* the opportunity to choose a memento.

"I'll take that!" she said, pointing at a life-sized stuffed cow, price tag $6,000. Monaco has gotten to her; it's those kiddie birthday parties on board 100-foot yachts that do it.

"Sorry, kid, the Jap in front of me just bought the last one."

She settled for a small plastic rabbit and I took her up to my favorite Parisian square, Place du Tertre, near the Sacre Coeur. The sidewalk portraitists lay in wait, and they descended upon us en masse when they saw my little girl; easy prey, they imagined.

In front of the Sacre Coeur, with all of Paris below us, Jean Piero grinded an organ and croaked froggy tunes while his monkey danced and Algerian street peddlers hawked snakeskin wallets, costume jewelry, their sisters.

"Change money?" whispered a casually dressed Frenchman. "Seven francs for the dollar."

"What is this, Poland? Buzz off."

* * *

The bottom for Paris is this: big city Frenchmen *are* smiling more; and so they should, with the prices they charge. A morning coffee and croissant at a corner café on Rue Rivoli set me back six bucks, the price of eggs, bacon, pancakes, juice and coffee back at Perkins Pancakes.

Standing in line at Orly's check-in desk, someone grabbed me from behind and whooped, "How ya doin', ya big hunk of burnin' love!'' I turned around and saw the sweetest sight Paris could offer: Miss Katie, in transit from Texas back home to Monaco, two weeks earlier than expected. She couldn't wait to get back to Le Texan. And neither could I.

16

Le Texan had been closed for two weeks—"Gone Fishing" said a sign in the window—and it felt like two months to the Monaco Cool crowd.

Richie the barkeep, from Pennsylvania, poured out a couple draft beers for Juan and me. I'd met Juan, a Spaniard, only an hour earlier when Monsieur Molass introduced us at Hotel Le Siecle. Juan was in Monaco, his first time, on business, and I could sense he needed to unstress; grow into a Monaco Cool frame of mind.

Within minutes of taking a stool at the Alamo Bar, Juan went from Mr. Nerveball to Señor Nirvana. His latino looks qualified him for a Miss Katie kiss on his first visit, record time, and the joint jumped with mariachi music and characters.

Shorty was sneaking around, doing his Houdini routine. He radiates success in his little jacket and tie. You ask him what he does, and he replies "consultant" or "in PR." Sometimes he's with Prince Albert, tagging a few steps behind, and when he's not, he's trying to cultivate cute young things for the two of them.

"Jailbait," whispered Crazy George once, envious as hell and hard up for a schtoink.

But the real problem with Shorty is this: he likes to

wine and dine you, then disappear when the check arrives. He'll spend 15 minutes in the wizzer. Then if he sees the check still isn't settled, he slinks around to the far end of the bar, near the bust of General Custer, and hangs tight behind a stool till the *cost* is clear. Then pops up and says, "What? It's already *paid?* How could you—it was *my* treat!"

Tony has caught on. Now he patiently awaits Shorty's reappearance from the join and thrusts *l'addition* into his small palm and says, "Lookin' for *this?*"

Crazy George plopped down on a stool, folded his arms on the bar and laid his head on top sideways, grinning painfully in my direction. This is a guy with a natural grin. He could lose a million bucks on a bum commodities deal and there would still be that grin. On this night, it was a distressed grin, like a child covering an urge to cry.

"Life is a very funny thing," said George.

We waited for more, Juan and I. But there was nothing more.

Poor George couldn't handle two weeks of no Le Texan. Sure, I'd gone to Paris, ran the Ritz Gauntlet, and that broke it up. But George kept his hectic pace, between commodities and Jimmy'z, and had no Alamo Bar at which to mellow out, catch up with himself.

Bubbly Sara Jane bounced in, excited about landing a job at Funnyville U, where Crazy George teaches. Sara Jane fell in love with Monaco while on sabbatical from Harvard, and even considered barkeep duty at Le Texan as a way to remain, tenure be damned.

But the occasion was sullied by a *faux pas* she'd pulled an hour earlier at the snooty Irish Library. Sara Jane had been talking with someone when Prince Albert sauntered over to say hello. "Oh, hello," she had quickly replied, then finished her sentence with the other person. When she turned back a second later, the Prince was gone, ushered away, all glaring eyes upon the "prince snubber."

"Don't sweat it," I told Sara Jane. "It was more polite to finish your sentence. You're an American. We don't bow to royalty. We only bend over for fanatical Iranians."

"But what should I do?" she pleaded. People in Monaco get into an awful tizzy about matters of royal protocol.

"For a start, sit down and have a shot of tequila," I counseled. "Then, don't do anything, except have another tequila if you still feel like doing something. If the Carabinieri don't turn up at your door by 6am, you're probably okay. If they *do* turn up, we didn't have this conversation."

Roberto sauntered in, hands on his hips, and took a good look around. It was a slow night for virgins at Le Texan and he sidled up to Sara Jane.

"We should do more together," said Roberto.

"We're already doing too much," she replied.

* * *

Richie pressed one too many *pressions*, draft beer, and I paid for it next morning. The hill up to my office at Le Siecle was steeper than usual and this meant stopping for cappucino at every café along Rue Princess Caroline.

First, a good frothy cup, with a croissant, at the Green Dolphin. Pickleman was there, studiously reading his morning papers and watching me recuperate out the corner of his eye.

"Haven't ya heard, Jake?" I growled. "Le Texan reopened."

"Has it? Oh. Hum. Yes." He looked left and right, up and down, back into his paper

After my third coffee, I was a case of "cappucino nerves," a state akin to being Italian. Winston had crossed his caffeine limit while he was here, unaccustomed to a cappucino's strength, and he nearly jumped out of his skin. I knew he'd had enough when I approached his table outside the Café de Paris and saw him scribbling madly into a little notebook. He looked up, and the intensity of his racing mind beamed through his eyes, as if he'd just snorted two toots of amphetamine-laced coke.

"I've got some great ideas we *must* talk about!" he hollered, trying to disengage the words faster than his mouth was prepared to deliver, his pores unleashing a torrent of perspiration. "Now!"

He sweated out the buzz. Next time I saw him he was drinking hot chocolate.

As for Don Juan, the Spaniard hung out every night at the Alamo Bar, growing Monaco Cooler by the hour. He traded a business suit and tightly-knotted tie for an open-neck *Faconnable* denim shirt; a briefcase for a foxy Australian blond, and returned to Madrid so Monaco Cool he was practically cryogenic.

17

The Pickleman was at the Alamo Bar, sipping red wine, unusually talkative. He shook his head, glanced this way and that, and spoke.

"Monaco," he said. "It's programmed to get people into trouble."

"Come again?"

"There's a web of temptation in this town. And just about everyone gets caught."

"What kind of web?"

"Take marriages. I've been here 10 years, and I've seen every kind of marriage break up before my eyes. The women are always searching for a richer man. Yeah, there's a lot of unhappiness here. A lot of unhappiness in money. The *nouveau-riche* are the absolute worst. They don't have any discipline. Old wealth grew up with responsibility. They can handle the burden. The *nouveau riche* break under the pressure, and that's what this town is full of."

"Broken *nouveau-riches?*"

"No, broken marriages," said the Pickleman. "They find that money doesn't buy happiness. If I woke up a millionaire, this is the last place I'd live. And Bicker agrees."

"But Bicker *is* a millionaire *and* he lives here."

"Sure, that's part of his PR show," said the Pickleman. "He *has* to live here. But he agrees. If you've got a Lamborghini, a Ferrari and a 30-foot yacht, someone's got *two* Lamborghinis, *two* Ferraris and a *40-foot* yacht. You look like small fry here no matter how much you have. Everyone's always trying to outdo each other."

"But you just said it *can't* be done?"

"Yes, but they don't *know* it, these stupid *nouveau-riches*. They try anyway."

"So, what keeps you here, Jake?"

The Pickleman looked every which way, then whispered, "Can't move. Just the thought of sending new address notices to all my clients worldwide is a daunting task."

"In your line of work, I bet you know some interesting stories, eh Jake?"

"Oh, yeah," he grinned, and when he does this, his tight, narrow face looks like a skull. He put his elbow on the bar, looked up and down, right and left, and lowered his voice, eyes flickering with excitement. "I was in Czechoslovakia once. Had dinner at a restaurant and met a man and his wife, they asked me to join them. The guy told me he worked for Radio Free Europe in Munich, broadcasting to the Czechs in their native language. He had a great looking wife. A few weeks later, back home, I read in the Herald Tribune that this guy defected to the communists. So I sat down and wrote a three-page letter to Radio Free Europe to tell them about my chance meeting with their ex-employee and mentioned that I'd given the guy my business card. They wrote back a nice letter saying the guy was bad news, but not to worry about him having my card."

The Pickleman paused.

"And?" I asked.

"That's it," he shrugged. "I didn't have to worry."

Bob Bicker walked in with a young twinkie on his arm, a 19 year-old English girl he'd picked up that afternoon on the "Rivieria Route" from London. The Pickleman joined them on the terrace and launched into his spook spiel, attempting to convince the girl that he was the guy who inspired Ian Fleming. Since they seemed to hit it off, Bicker suggested that he retire home and *they* journey further into the night together. The Pickleman was petrified at the notion, white-faced and trembling, but the girl chose wealth over intrigue and split with Bicker.

Bhaman was out on the terrace, too. He, the Iranian who almost dropped his drawers on my behalf while haggling with French Customs.

"You can grow lazy in Monaco," said Bhaman, lazing back in his chair. "Be careful."

He was referring *not* to the Monaco Cool crowd, but to the Motion People, the Monaco Bored. You ask the Motion People—like Lyin' Leon—what they're doing, and they tell you what they're *planning*. And they're constantly tugging at you to become one of them, kind of like *Invasion of the Body Snatchers*. Leon's latest recruit is Rascasse Rupert, a fast-talking Old Etonian who rasps authoritatively, but has cultivated Leon's penchant for the grand whopper.

If youth is wasted on the young, Monaco is wasted on the old and rich. The Motion People have lost their sense of mission, reduced spiritually to searching for a better cappucino.

When a suicide occurs, it is usually a member of the Motion People, consumed by lethargy or gambling debts. Carabinieri Control does not approve of suicide, so they play a little game called "Move the Corpse to France." If you jump from the top floor of the Millefiore, Monaco's tallest building, they find your body in Menton, five miles away.

* * *

Le Texan is so Monaco Cool that even with Prince Albert as a regular, Carabinieri Control has put the place on their *hit list*. It started with the neighbors, who called to complain about the loud whoopee. They don't like mariachi music coming up through their wooden floor boards past midnight. Real party poops.

"This isn't the wild west!" they shout over the wire.

Yes it is, you old bag, and if you don't believe me, c'mon down for an upside-down margarita!

Then the old farts upstairs started dropping water bombs onto the canopy covering the terrace, and one burst through, not 10 feet from where I was sitting. The police came, not to investigate attempted murder, but to grumble again about "American" rowdiness. The bombing was pawned off as Monegasque neighbors will be Monegasque neighbors.

But if Le Texan was in danger, it was from neither Carabinieri Control nor Monegasque neighbors. Much worse. It looked, from where I was standing, next to Custer, that the Alamo Bar had met its Santa Anna.

It came in the form of Monk, a big, brawny man-Friday to Isaac Tigrett who, having sold his stake in the Hard Rock Cafe, appeared to be moving in on Monaco. A month earlier Isaac had bought Shorty's tiny stake in Le Texan. All Shorty ever did was try to schtoink teeny-boppers by merit of his part-ownership, a totally hands-off approach (except for the girls). But Isaac had other plans, installing Monk behind the bar and, with him, an invisible sign on the wall that said: "Under New Management (or will be soon)."

Monk's first confrontation, in front of everyone, was with Tony. He wanted to change the Alamo Bar's margarita recipe. Next, he insisted on pushing a paper napkin beneath every drink and beer bottle. ("What is this, Monte Carlo?") I'd scrunch mine up, toss it aside and... swish, another appeared in less than 10 seconds.

18

The view from my front balcony includes a long stretch of Italian coastline. Sometimes in late afternoon, with Monaco cast in shadow, this hilly peninsula is bathed in fiery orange sunlight. And on a clear, crisp night, its twinkling lights beg you to come on out.

The temptation proved overwhelming during Winston's visit. I'd driven him across the border to look at Italy up close and we searched for the glittery, inviting resort. We'd meant to stop for lunch, maybe a bowl of linguini carbonara and a bottle of Soave at one of the many ristorantes that I *knew* would decorate the promenade. We found the stretch. We did not find a promenade bustling with open air cafés. Up close, the mirage consisted of a cracked concrete path, a row of dilapidated buildings and a lonely, dirty beach strewn with jagged rock and garbage. If someone showed me a picture of this place, I'd guess it was Bulgaria.

We didn't stop for lunch, not even cappucino. Winston took one good eyeful and screamed, "Get me outta here!" The view from my window would never be the same.

I hadn't planned to return to Italy any time soon, or later, but a trip to the mad republic with my family became necessary. Our 90-day ration for staying in France was due to expire; our passports needed a fix.

We could have flown to Geneva. We *should* have flown to Geneva. But our predicament coincided with April Fool's Day, so Italy was the obvious choice. The joke, inevitably, was on us.

An Italian banker advised me to steer clear of Torino, Genoa and every place else I suggested. So we listened to him and aimed the Jeep toward Camoghli, which he described as a quaint fishing village-turned-resort the other side of Genoa.

Road signs on the *autostrada* are jumbled together. By the time you catch a passing glimpse of your route, you're too late. This, and all the honking, is how Italians are trained to be highly strung.

I accidentally, stupidly, exited the *autostrada* at Genoa and found there was no way to get back on. From a distance, this port city is quite attractive; in fact, the further the better, because with a ringside seat you see it for the architectural nightmare it is: a grimy, polluted, mad frenzy of withering tenements, hanging laundry and smokestacks belching dark clouds of noxious gas. It is the kind of place that makes you wish you had stayed home. Even if home is Staten Island.

The bypass road ended abruptly and we were spilled into Genoa's center. Traffic snarled hopelessly as five lanes converged into one, Italian drivers cursing and beeping their little Fiats incessantly, refusing to yield, both their honor and manhood at stake. Two archaic public buses made a sandwich of my Jeep and farted up a storm of brown leaded fumes. We were well and truly schtoinked.

It took but 30 seconds to realize we'd made a big mistake coming to Camoghli. It started with the hotel, Camoghli's best, *Cenabio Dei Dogi* (Spielberg gets his names from an Italian hotel directory). A grubby little man with dirty clothes and several teeth greeted us on the Dogi's forecourt. A similar character led us into an elevator stinking of *very* ripe Camembert that ascended with us to a dark, musty hall. Large clusters of open-ended pipes protruded from the wall above the entrance to each room. The room, reminiscent of *Psycho*, came with a price tag of $275 per night. You need a sense of humor to visit Italy.

We told Paolo at the check-in desk that we'd think about it, and asked him to point us toward the nicest part of town. This turned out to be a stretch of cracked concrete, a row of dilapidated buildings and a beach strewn with jagged rocks. Everything around us was rotting or had already rotted. As we looked westward down the coastline toward Genoa and beyond, we contemplated the uncontemplatable. Then we jumped into the jeep, thumbed our nose at the *Dogi* and whipped *around* Genoa at top speed, through mountain tunnels toward Sanremo, not 25 miles from Monaco.

We took a room at the five-star Hotel Royal, a member of Leading Hotels of the World and reputed to be the finest inn on the Italian Riviera.

Our room was decorated in flowery pink wallpaper and pea-green curtains and carpet; illumination courtesy of a naked lightbulb. I switched on the TV and there it was again: "I Dream of Jeannie." This time Jeannie and the colonel were speaking Italian, and if the original English had been as dramatic, both would have won Emmys.

We went down to breakfast after a long, uncomfortable night featuring a soft mattress and hard pillows. Important rule of thumb: if breakfast is included in the price, you probably won't like it.

The cream-jacketed and bow-tied waiters pranced about directionless, serving croissants made from flaked cardboard and cappucino that tasted like botched Nescafé.

"Thank you *very* much," I said to the waiter.

"Nothing," he replied, which precisely described my tip.

"Do you speak English?" I asked.

"No, I practice," he said.

"Then practice this: take coffee and give chef enema, *Si?*"

"*Si, grazie.*"

The Royal *is* the finest hotel on the Italian Riviera. And this explains why the most pleasing sight in Italy is the last sign pointing to *Francia*.

19

onaco's ruling Grimaldi family is of Genovese extraction, and they probably thank God each night they don't live in Genoa. I do.

The Principality has been in the family since 1297 when a buccaneer named Francois "The Spiteful" staged a coup. It was a classic sting. He dressed as a Franciscan monk and knocked at the palace gates, feigning hunger. Sympathetic guards opened up, and they were the first stung, skewered by Francis with a sword he pulled from beneath his smock. Grimaldi warriors, lurking in the bushes, rushed the fortress and rousted the ruling Spinolas, a rival Genovese family. No mortgage application, nothing. *And* you could call yourself *Prince*.

Monaco was not always the Palm Beach of Europe. In fact, it barely got by until the mid-1800s when the Grimaldis decided to hustle up some action. Until then, they had filled their time bumping off one another and hanging out with royalty in Paris and Vienna. They decided to lease Monaco's deep water port to the Russians for a hundred years, and actually negotiated a deal. But the French and Italians kicked up a fuss, and the Grimaldis were forced to dream up another moneymaking scheme. Someone hit on casino gambling, and a quiet corner of the Principality was christened Monte Carlo and transformed into a gambler's paradise. They almost called it Albertville, after the first Prince Albert.

The new casino literally put Monte Carlo on the map; so much so, that even today, when you say Monaco, and not Monte Carlo, people think you're talking about Morocco.

European cash gushed in, and with it, the wealthy, the famous and, synonymously, a reputation for decadence. Training along the Riviera, an unamused Queen Victoria would draw her curtains as she passed through the Principality.

When Grace Kelly, a young, beautiful actress from Philadelphia entered the Grimaldi family in the mid-20th century, Monegasques did not immediately open their hearts. Today, they revere her memory. Grace anchored her new family to the Principality rather than follow the Grimaldi tradition of ruling mostly in absentia. Some whisper that it was her father's generous dowry that helped transform Monaco from a declining gambling den and Mediterranean backwater into a vibrant, profitable glamour capital.

Grace personally supervised the constant redevelopment in the Principality with an eye for style that ensured improvements were truly that. Many of the concrete and glass eyesores constructed since her death would not have survived her scrutiny. It was Princess Grace who insisted upon a hands-on approach for keeping goodness in and badness out, and she nurtured a cultural growth that is her legacy.

Prince Rainier rules, some whisper, with a penchant for pettiness and remote supremacy. He is shy, mistrustful—it is whispered—and lonely.

Prince Albert, also shy, takes seriously the family business, and especially enjoys interviewing prospective candidates for princess.

Out of such interviews has grown The Royal Destiny Phenomenon, which works like this: Prince Albert meets a stunning blue-eyed blond—always in the image of his mother—during a stateside visit, conducts an interview, and graciously suggests that she visit him in Monaco. The girl quits her job, blows her savings on a new wardrobe and arrives in the Principality, expecting a romantic week with Prince Charming. Each one uniformly believes it is her *destiny* to tie the knot with a prince, become a princess and live happily-ever-after inside a fairy-tale. This is what she tells her friends; often, the *National Enquirer* gets wind of her song and dance and proclaims an engagement, a "world exclusive." Sometimes it evolves into erotomania. The result is a let-down of royal proportions: she gets a few hours with the Prince, maybe a ride in his beamer, with all its fancy hi-tech doo-dahs, and a *few days* with Shorty, or worse, Roberto.

Le Texan's story is shorter by about 690 years.

In a burst of inspiration, Prince Rainer gave the place its name, and Le Texan opened its cactus green doors in the spring of '88, one week before the Grand Prix, Monaco's premier sporting event.

Ma Kelly had bought the place a couple of years earlier and ran it the way she found it, as a pizzeria called Vesuvio; but soon found herself being run by an uppity French chef who came with the kitchen and would not answer to anyone, least of all a woman, and an *American* woman to boot.

Vesuvio grew too hot, and Ma Kelly called Texas for help. Mike and Kate bounded over. Kate saw it as a temporary assignment; a good reason to take time off from a strained marriage. Fate had other ideas.

Miss Katie sized up the haughty chef, determined the kitchen wasn't big enough for the both of them, and ordered his ass out by sundown. Then, in a moment of madness, remodeled the premises into a hacienda with stippled walls, red-tile floor, wood-beamed ceiling, long-horn skulls and assorted cacti. Kate washed out the stable of stale staff and hired a slew of youthful, doe-eyed waitresses— Miss Katie's girls. The long Alamo Bar, constructed against the advice of every French bank manager, soon became the hub of Monaco Cool.

* * *

My daughter was the only American at the American International School, a U.N. mix predominated by Brits, and her schoolwork was equally curious. One day she was doodling dollar signs; another, she announced she'd been learning about "taxes." What else would you expect in Monaco?

Halfway through the year an English busybody I call the Slag conspired to oust the school marm, Molly Brown, an elderly Mary Poppins.

The Slag epitomizes the low class Brit who parades around the Principality in four-inch Chanel earrings and pretends to be related to the Queen's wiper. But to anyone with an ounce of sense she looks like a 20-dollar blow with a horse face and horse's ass.

Americans believe in everyone getting their day in court. But Brits prefer a devious approach—anything, however sneaky, to avoid a fuss. And the Slag, lobbying furtively, managed to get Molly fired with only three days' notice.

Molly Brown took her case to the six and seven year-olds. "I have to leave," she told them, "because your mommies and daddies don't like me."

And then, ignoring her dismissal, Molly appeared for work on the fourth day, and no one knew quite what to do, least of all the Brits, who, horrors, sensed a *scene*! The other teachers gasped and the kids cheered. And it looked like my favorite course, Anarchy 101, had been introduced to the curriculum, a counter-balance to dollar signs and taxes.

The Slag went into a desperate panic, 'phoning parents and demanding they swear depositions trashing Molly's worth as a human being. The Slag's tongue is too big for her mouth, and you could hear it, sloshing around, obstructing her venomous diatribe, words fighting to erupt through horse lips and popping out like bathtub farts.

Molly held her own throughout the week, oblivious to the furor, or simply not caring. Then one morning the headmaster from Nice arrived and pulled a George Wallace, physically barring Molly's entry.

Choked up, Molly refused a lift home from a sympathetic parent. "I need to walk," she said, fighting tears. Molly Brown, irrepressible till now, disappeared down the street.

20

When the U.S. Navy hits town, the streets of Monaco's "friendly port" turn ugly. They park their gray warships outside the sea wall and launch a landing craft shuttle. Not to be confused with shuttle diplomacy. These guys are a *setback* to diplomatic relations between the United States and Europe.

Our first line of defense on the quay are the ratdogs. They booby trap the pavement with deadly wet clarts. The first wave of navy shoes take a beating, but the sailors keep coming in droves, and the poor ratdogs can't keep pace.

Within a couple of hours, the streets of Condamine are packed with strolling, gawking sailors. They whistle and hoot at French women, shake the orange trees and yell "Yo!" to attract a waiter's attention.

They come from all parts of the States, though they look and sound like under-programmed robots, off the same assembly-line.

The barstools at the Alamo Bar were removed to accommodate an occupation. Monk tried to keep the peace, pecs bulging beneath a Le Texan tee-shirt—a hot item—but the navy turned the joint into a war zone anyway, and even Jaws put in a cameo appearance. One sailor half-emptied a bottle of Bordeaux in one swig, then tossed his tacos on the

103

bar; another spewed up like a fountain on the terrace. "I ain't havin' what *he* ate!" said one navy wit. Another sailor tried to hose down the bathroom wall grafitti with his dick.

The Alamo Bar was three deep with nuclear weapons technicians, all racing to get drunk, fall down, stagger up and have another drink.

I jumped in and made some fast friends which, like fast food, comes in styrofoam and stays warm for three minutes. It became apparent too quick they had nothing to say you couldn't learn from "Leave it to Beaver" reruns. Oh, they're quite happy to talk about nuclear engineering to anyone who'll listen to them spout off about warheads and capabilities, but since I'm not KGB, I move on down the bar.

The Pickleman walked in and was aghast by the sight of wall-to-wall drunken robotoids. He would have left, but Miss Katie pecked him on the cheek, snapping his gherkin to attention, and the P'man hung out for a glass of *vin rouge* while navy "yahoos!" reverberated the joint.

Roberto sauntered in—and practically ran out. And someone pinned a picture of Shorty on the toilet wall with a caption that read: "This man wanted, preferably maimed, for saying John Paul Jones was a faggot."

* * *

The Pickleman leapt from his jar at the Green Dolphin and rushed out to flag my attention. He looked both ways, ran a forefinger up and down his nose, and poised himself to deliver a briefing.

"Voodoo," said the P'man, attempting an expression even more serious than usual. "Voodoo," he repeated. "I'm on a case involving voodoo. It's hush-hush. I can't talk about it."

"I understand, Jake."

"You see," he continued. "I've been retained by this multimillionaire in California who's involved in a messy divorce. Real messy. His ex-wife is French and she belongs to a voodoo cult and...I'd better not say anymore."

"Okay, Jake. I understand."

"No, you don't. He's been in the hospital twice for operations 'cos they're sticking pins into voodoo dolls with his picture on them. It's fucking terrible. He finds these wax dolls under the furniture in his house. The maids go berserk when they see these things. And it works! Shit! First he had his dick operated on. Yeah, his *dick*! Then the dog died after he found a dog doll with a pin in its heart. Now it's his eyes. He just got out of the hospital again. He can hardly see. The last doll had pins in the eyes. Those beasts. He called me just last week and I asked him how he felt. He yelled, 'How, the fuck do you think I feel, I'm almost blind!' Yeah, this is for real."

"That's pretty bizarre, Jake. What are you doing about it?"

"Oh, I can't talk about *that*. Confidential. I don't work on the overt side, you know. I'm *covert*. There's a difference, you know. Damn lawyers. They don't know anything about covert. It takes a covert guy like me to find things out."

"What have you found out?"

"Are you kidding? I've got a file *this thick*," said the Pickleman, indicating two inches with his thumb and forefinger. "Want to see it?"

Assuming he meant the file, I nodded yes and we agreed to meet the following day.

The P'man's voodoo dossier, presented to me over cappucino at the Green Dolphin, consisted of a photo copied, year-old article from the LA Times magazine. That was all.

"What I need to know are two things," whispered the P'man. "Is this voodoo cult considered a criminal organization? That's very important. And does it have a French connection?"

"Aha," I said. "What leads do you have?"

"None at the moment."

I scanned the magazine article.

"Why don't you 'phone the reporter who wrote this?" I asked.

"Hmmm. Hadn't thought of that."

"And there's a Cuban expert mentioned here, in the Miami area. Have you called him?"

"Hmmm. No."

The Pickleman had been contemplating his "file" for six months, waiting for the answers to smack him across the face.

Concerned suddenly about his credentials, the P'man plucked from his wallet a membership card for some kind of industrial security association. I looked at it.

"How long did you say you were in the State Department?" I asked.

He looked right and left, ran a forefinger up and down his nose, and whispered, "three years, security" in one short burst.

"They must have been sorry to lose you."

The Pickleman nodded, affirmatively.

21

The drive from Monaco to Nice is always a pleasure, especially along the *basse corniche*, the coastal route. It takes you through the picturesque towns of Beaulieu and Villefranche and, with the tranquil Med on your left and mountains on your right, and Tom Waits brawling his way through a tune, we're talking 40 minutes of magic.

The only thing you have to watch for are Italian tags, particularly if they're moving. These babies pull out, cut in, and do it fast, with no warning. And whenever they stop, they stop for no reason, because if there's a reason, they don't bother. And even when they stop, their brake lights don't work.

Moono had been on a plane for 13 hours but, clad in bright orange sports pants and a Glacier National Park tee-shirt, he was ready to inject his unique character into the mix. Moono was the best undercover stingman in the IRS, investigating everything from money-laundering in Switzerland to brothels in Nevada, and when I told the Pickleman he was coming out to visit, the P'man practically jerked his gherkin on the spot.

I took Moono to the open-air market for cappucino just in time to see the Mad Market Man go bananas. This deranged Al Capone look-alike hangs around the flower stalls, near an entrance to the in-door part of the market. Every few minutes he walks inside; suddenly, for no explainable reason, his jaw drops, his eyes pop out and he freezes in his tracks. Then—encouraged by nearby marketeers—he yells and thrashes his arms wildly, in a 15-second spurt, then turns 'round and walks back outside. The Mad Market Man, obviously Monegasque, repeats this performance two or three times daily, always at 11am.

Awaiting me at home was an urgent message from the Pickleman: "Something's come up—Green Dolphin at noon." I took Moono along, and the P'man took to him instantly.

"I'm covert," said the Pickleman, for the fifth time in five minutes. "I take the 'pretext approach.' You know what that means, Moono, eh? Heh, heh." He looked over his shoulder in one quick motion, readjusted his seat and bent over a cappucino. "I know how it's done," he whispered. "What I need is *clients*."

Moono's first new acquaintance at the Alamo Bar was Googer. Steven Googer. Half Hungarian, part American, all nutcase—with a cheshire cat grin, frizzy red hair receding two-thirds back and Son of Sam eyes.

"It's all a matter of percentages," says Googer, expounding on women. "I hit on 20 a day, three respond."

The Pickleman, unusually relaxed, joined us at the bar. "It's been a busy day," he sighed. "London's been on to me all afternoon." He looked right, left, ran a forefinger up and down his nose, and launched into a spiel about *covert* this and *covert* that, and it's a dirty job with no credit, but *somebody's* got to do it, and that's why he spends his life coverting.

"Pass the baked beans," I said to Katie as she passed by, "so's I can contribute to this conversation."

"Do your work, do it well and fuck 'em," muttered the P'man, and then he grumbled some more, about the "backbiting Brits."

"Yeah," he said, into his second glass of *rouge*, "I was trained by the Brits, and devious bastards they are. Intelligence, you know. Covert. That's where I learned to be devious. Most people shy away from me. I'm covert. People don't understand. If I operated in the U.S., like you Moono, I'd be locked up in a week."

The Pickleman's happiest days, he told Moono, were with the U.S. Marines at Camp Pendleton where he was a drill instructor. He demonstrated by hopping off his barstool and snapping to attention. He was trained to be a U.S. embassy guard though, thank God, was never assigned to protect an embassy.

I sat back and watched the P'man shoot his wad. Some old admiral, the U.S. Navy's local big *fromage*, held court nearby over a fajitas dinner party. Then Princess Caroline walked in with an entourage.

"That's Princess Caroline!" yelled the Pickleman to Moono. "Pssst," he motioned to Richie the barkeep. "Princess Caroline is out there!"

Only a few of us know that Richie is Caroline's cousin, and that did not include the P'man, who is never in the know about anything. Rich gazed at the P'man with a blank stare that said: utter contempt.

And the Pickleman was all excited because Caroline's presence meant that her *bodyguards* would be nearby, and the P'man loves bodyguards.

Shorty whizzed around the place, checking his watch like the rabbit in *Alice in Wonderland*, waiting for a tab to be settled. Roberto moseyed in, hands on hips, curls glistening, and sidled up to a new waitress from New Zealand. "Stick with me and you'll be safe," he told her.

Then Crazy George joined us at the bar.

"What do you do here?" Moono asked.

"Schtoink all the good-looking ladies," said George.

"And after that?"

"Well, then there's all the bad-looking ones..."

"Pssst." A young Englishman at a table near the bar

leaned over and tried to summon the Pickleman's attention. "Pssst!"

The P'man ignored the intrusion, in the midst of revealing to us his nickname: Wrong-way Yennie.

"Pssst!" the Englishman called again. "How's the spook business?"

The Pickleman twisted right and left uneasily, threw his right hand up over his eyes, then down again, and flashed a look of unusual self-confidence at his tormentor. "Stick your dick in it!" he hollered, inspired to new heights by Moono's presence.

The Pickleman turned back toward us. "Yeah, Wrong-way Yennie. That's what the locals called me when I lived in Greece because whenever tourists asked me directions, I'd send 'em the wrong way. I do the same thing now. Especially with the Krauts and the Italians. They ask me the way to the casino and I point them up the Rock."

* * *

Lyin' Leon reappeared at the Green Dolphin after a four-month hiatus in North America. That's the thing about Monaco: everyone's always coming and going. I was sitting with Moono and the Pickleman when Leon walked in, not two hours off a plane.

"Yeah, fixed those thieving bastards," Leon started to brag. "Set up a trust in my wife's name on the Turks & Caicos. The rest is in Switzerland. That's still a *great* place to hide cash. So, what do you do, Moono?"

"I'm retired," said Moono. "Used to work for the government."

"Oh, post office or something?"

"No. IRS."

Leon gagged on his cappucino, turned red, purple, and looked like he was going to need a doctor.

"It's a mindless bureaucracy," continued Moono, softening the blow. "They never liked me, thought I was nuts, but couldn't get rid of me."

Leon relaxed a bit, and spent the next 20 minutes telling us about his new house in Arizona, his new Saab Turbo, and on and on.

* * *

Even though he worked for the IRS for 25 years, Moono couldn't come to terms with French money. This isn't unusual for Americans, for whom sterling is a kind of silver, yen is something we have once in a while for Chinese take-out and franc is the local barkeep. Americans think of foreign currency as a kind of play money you need to buy postcards, pay cabbies and for situations where plastic won't do nicely.

Swiss money is the best. Not because the Swiss are dead serious about it, but because their banknotes are decorated with faces of men who look like the forefathers of anarchism. One looks like Rasputin; another, like Abbie Hoffman.

22

The Pickleman was down in the dumps. His heart broke when he saw Moono off at the heliport. Moono had spent every night on a stool at Le Texan's Alamo Bar. I offered him all kinds of choices of places to go, and he'd say, "Unless you have a good reason for going some place else, I'd just as soon stay here." And the Pickleman was right there next to him, hanging on every word. The two of them, cutting quips like a couple of cavorting coverters, were a sight to behold—a sort of undercover Laurel and Hardy. Normally austere with a look of constipation, the Pickleman had come in from the cold, doffed his cloak and even spoofed his own spookiness.

But now, sitting inside the Dolphin, he looked austere and costive again, like a lost puppy dog pining for its master. Alone, again, in a covert world.

Lyin' Leon was getting on my nerves. All you want to do first thing in the morning is read the *Herald Tribune* and sip cappucino, and he sits down to deliver a discourse on all the money he lost by not buying Boeing stock, a million dollars' worth, 'cos his broker recommended against the transaction. You put the paper down to be polite and, swish, it no sooner hits the table then he grabs it to check the latest currency fluctuations. He runs 52 companies and won't buy his own paper.

A hundred thousand tourists—mostly Italians—were in town, or on their way, for the Grand Prix, and the Principality resembled a maximum security prison with 10-foot high mesh wire fences and road barriers everywhere. I'd woken up every morning the previous week feeling like a lab mouse trying to find my way around a maze. With each new day, a new barrier.

Fumes from leaded gasoline bonded with unfiltered cigarette smoke to create a yellowish haze that wouldn't budge.

All things considered, it seemed like a good time to get out of town.

The very thought of Switzerland made my lungs perk up. Fresh mountain air, obsessively clean unobstructed streets—and no one's likely to start a war.

Geneva is where world leaders meet to discreetly resolve their problems, within yodeling distance of the gnomes of Zurich, who finance the arms that inflame the problems.

There are more spooks per capita in Geneva than anywhere else in the world, cloaked by over a hundred international organizations that thrive upon creating problems everywhere else in the world. Those Geneva residents who crack jokes about Geneva's boring neutrality are invariably the ones running revolutions and counter-revolutions from afar.

Geneva, in a word, is *serene*. In other words, it is the exact opposite of Genoa. The city's landmark is not a building, like London's Big Ben or the Eiffel Tower in Paris, but a fountain called the *Jet d'Eau*, which shoots a spray of water 400-feet straight up at 120 miles an hour, meant to represent life's eternal ejaculation.

When you stand on the Mont Blanc Bridge and look

around, the panorama is rich. You know how on Times Square you have "SONY" and "Nikon" and other symbols of North American culture in bright lights? In Geneva you have 270 degrees of banks, all boldly announcing their presence in colorful neon. Bank Indosuez, Banque Multi-Commerciale, Hong Kong Bank of the Middle East, UOB Bank, ABN Bank, CIA bank, and on and on. Though it officially speaks three languages, French, German and Italian or *Gerfrilian*, Switzerland has only one state religion: Banking. The gnomes of Zurich are its priests and everyone is a believer. Converts from tin-pot Third World countries pour in daily to open numbered accounts, pray for more foreign aid and chant the old Swiss proverb: "Money may not make you happy, but it improves your style of misery."

The illuminated signs that don't belong to a bank, belong to the tick-tock industry. Patek-Phillippe, Blancpain, Audemars, Piaget, Raymond Weil, they're all here. The 90 degrees of panorama not filled with watchmakers and banks comprises of part lake view and part pastoral, hilly countryside dotted with handsome estates not ten minutes from downtown Geneva. This is where Mr. Patek and Mr. Blancpain and Mr. Weil live, along with all their banker buddies. The phrase "time is money" was coined in Geneva.

But the biggest gold mine in Serene City is McDonald's, where they churn out Big Macs faster than the rest of the city produces swatch watches.

If you sprang the golden arches in Teheran, it wouldn't matter if Salman Rushdie was the manager, they'd need marines, not to protect Sal and the burgers, but to keep an orderly line around the block.

Geneva was especially serene because we inadvertently arrived on a holiday and the shops were closed. This meant my wife couldn't go nuts, for at least a day, on all the elegant consumerables on display along Rue du Rhone. The Japs were reduced to taking pictures of everything they planned to buy. And judging from their camera angles, they had banks on their shopping lists, not Swiss Army Knives.

It didn't take long to sniff out Geneva's version of Le Texan. I worked at a brew, watching a pair of Mexican mariachis strafe the tables of Cafe Manana with "Aye yi-yi-yis," trying in vain to raise enthusiasm. The lights were too bright and the joint needed more than music. It needed characters. It needed Crazy George, Pickleman; even Shorty, sneaking around, pumping palms, doing his big-shot routine. Let's face it, I was homesick for Le Texan.

23

The day after the Grand Prix, Monaco looks like a neutron bomb was detonated. Property is intact, but the folks left behind are completely shattered. Monsieur Molass, leaning against his reception desk at Le Siecle, looked a near corpse. Bags beneath sunken eyes fell past his clipped moustache.

"What happened?" I already knew the answer. As a relatively inexpensive hotel across from the train station, his inn catered to the low end of the Grand Prix market. The scumbags. And they kept him hopping at the bar till five each morning.

"I haven't been home in five days," moaned Molass.

"You mean you slept in your own hotel?" I didn't mean this the way it sounded.

"Sleep?" said Molass.

The service company he had brought in earlier in the year had not lived up to his expectations and, with his shrewd sense of timing, Molass sacked them all, including his manager, a few days before the big race. Then the chef walked out in solidarity.

I left Molass to recover in peace and, too late for the Mad Market Man's 11am wig-out, I stopped at Cosilito's Condamine Café to grab lunch. The Mexican tried to fob me off with their special Grand Prix menu: same fare, three times the normal price.

"Get rid of this, Chiliman, and cook me one of your omelettes with everything in it."

* * *

"Who's that new guy behind the bar?" asked the Pickleman, referring to Monk who had already been around more than a month.

"He likes to be called 'Gorilla'," I said. "And if you tell him 'Isaac is an asshole', he'll like that and be your friend."

Monk loomed up, all chest and pecs. "What can I get ya, pardner?" he asked the P'man.

"Get me Richie."

Richie took the Pickleman's order for a glass of red wine, salvaged from someone else's undrunk bottle as specified by the P'man, and Monk was pissed off at the slight.

Later, Miss Katie came along, pecked the P'man on each cheek, and chided him for upsetting Monk.

"He's really a nice guy," said Kate, "and very good behind the bar."

"I suppose he reads Shakespeare, too," smirked the Pickleman.

Katie called to Monk and motioned him over. "Have you met Jake?" she said.

"He didn't want to meet *me*!" huffed Monk.

"Oh, it's got feelings," said the Pickleman, refusing to even look in Monk's direction. Miss Katie's attention was flagged elsewhere. "He finked on me!" hissed the Pickleman. "I *hate* finks. That's *another* reason I don't like him."

When the Pickleman got up to relieve his gherkin, Monk tried to give his barstool away.

Shorty was running around, all excited, looking like he owned the place. Earlier in the day he had telephoned Tony to make a booking. "I'm bringing a very important person in tonight," Shorty had said. "Ringo Starr. Let me have the best table, the one in the corner, for 10pm."

So here was Shorty, racing around at 9:30, looking important, making sure everything was set. Katie's brother Mike was hanging out at the bar; he couldn't have thought Ringo would actually show; Shorty's been stood up before, many times, but Mike takes no chances about missing a celebrity.

Ten o'clock came and went. No Ringo. Shorty sat at his corner table, glancing at his watch every two minutes and looking up excitedly whenever someone walked through the door. Ten-thirty and no Ringo. Shorty ordered dinner. Eleven o'clock and no Ringo. Shorty was still checking his watch.

Tony never had any doubt that Shorty would be dining alone. He'd seen it all before with a Liza Minelli booking, a Roger Moore booking, and other celebrities he meets dogging Prince Albert.

Shorty arrived in Monaco three years before with a pretty wife and a couple of step-daughters, and was immediately smitten by the testosterone tick Pickleman yelps about. Mrs. Shorty saw this and decreed the Principality unfit for family stability. She packed their bags.

"But Albert needs me!" cried Shorty, who had assigned himself the role of royal fishmonger.

It had nothing to do with mid-life crisis. One day he's living in Arizona, just another short person, consultant, in

PR, it doesn't matter, all three. Suddenly, he's sidekick to a *real* prince, rubs shoulders with tennis pros, film celebrities and pop stars, and he's surrounded by beautiful models, many of whom think he's a path to the prince. You think he's going back to Arizona?

After months and months, the Pickleman finally noticed Shorty.

"You know that little guy with the moustache?" asked the P'man. "He was here the other night with Prince Albert, sitting with him, talking for a long time. Then, another night, he was here with a couple beautiful women. Who *is* this guy?" The Pickleman is some private dick.

Googer walked in, cheshire cat grin, arm outstretched— "Hi, I'm Googer!"—piercing eyes. Miss Katie stopped to say hello. Googer touched her cheek and let his fingers drop to her neck. Sensitive to the touch, she recoiled, and Googer said something about strangulation; something like, "People who fear being strangled can die from just a mere touch."

"Do you know this from experience?" I asked.

Googer didn't answer.

"I've learned a lesson today," bellowed Crazy George, pulling up a stool. "I've got no fucking balls!"

I whipped out my notebook; this was a choice quote.

"You can quote me on that," yelled George. "I don't have the fucking balls to trade commodities. If I don't make any money soon, I'm out of it!"

The Pickleman watched me scribble and asked, "Are you writing a book?"

"Why? You want to play yourself in the movie?"

24

I went looking for Mickey Rourke at the Cannes Film Festival. All I found were a lot of hypists and hucksters doing their weirdness along the Croisette. I wanted to pull a Shorty. You now, shoot the shit with Mickey, drop Albert's name and phone Tony for a booking at Le Texan.

Inside the Carlton Hotel, independent producers—*independent* being a euphemism for *unemployed*—were dressed like Don Johnson and talking about *doing* lunch, putting people on the map and hustling, hustling, hustling for that ever elusive finance. Someone to foot the bill for an "I'm-gonna-make-ya-a-star!" lifestyle.

These guys are the fastest talkers in the world, and the less they know, the more authoritatively they speak. And they reek of the kind of sincerity you haven't seen since Captain Kangaroo. Each one has an Oscar-winner just waiting to be shot, if only some investor would fork over five mil to play with. The first 500K pays for their Polo lounge breakfasts, suites at the Pierre and trans-Atlantic Concording while they leverage another five mil.

Cannes is great for watching the French, a people who supposedly worship their language, but who are crazy about adorning themselves in English. They wear shirts, sweaters and sweatshirts embroidered or printed with nonsensical phrases like "Navy Arctic" and "Best Montana" and "Delicious Pig." French youth goes nuts over everything American, the '50s-look mostly, like Levi 501s and Dexter penny loafers.

Unfortunately, the salespersons are still French, even if all their wares are American; pouting bitches who grow huffy at the slightest provocation. And just walking in and saying *bon jour* with an American accent provokes them. In the States you can return a shirt after wearing it for two months and they'll apologize for the inconvenience and give you a cash refund. In France, forget about a refund. Forget about an exchange. Even if you haven't unwrapped your purchase, it's yours forever. The saleswoman who reluctantly spoke perfect English when making the sale now remembers only one word: "No."

* * *

I finally got invited out to The Villa. The way everyone at the Alamo Bar jabbers about Isaac Tigrett's *Villa Mimosa* on Cap D'Ail, you'd think it was the only villa on the Cote d'Azur.

In Isaac's absence, Monk runs the manor as Le Texan's country cousin. I got tapped to attend a party he threw for the staff because I'm around more than some of the waitresses.

From the terrace pool, warmed to 80 degrees, a moonlit seascape soothes cappucino nerves while the lights of St. Jean-Cap Ferrat flicker in the distance. The ultra hi-tech CD cranks out tunes and Monk, a gracious host, sees to it that everyone has a libation. And if you're there, pulling on a brew, congratulations, 'cos you're among the coolest crowd in town.

By day, The Villa gets down to business. And business, under Monk's personal supervision, is pumping iron. Richie is building up his arms, Mike, his legs, the waitresses, their bazongas, and Hootenanny George, anything that'll stop shaking for a minute. Prince Albert wants to get cracking too, if he can give Shorty the slip.

* * *

Bob Bicker was back in town, hanging out by day at Miami Beach Club and by night at the Alamo Bar, tended to at both venues by the Pickleman. He got the P'man boozed on *rouge* one night and horny for a woman. Tried all the young ladies in sight, and all the old ones, too, but couldn't score.

One of Richie's six girlfriends, a stunning six-foot blond model strolled in, wearing a sexy pout.

"Let me handle this," said Bicker, rising to his full five feet and rolling up his sleeves to display the diamond-studded Rolex and chunky gold bracelets.

"Hello!" said Bicker to the blond, in his lowest, most virile voice. "*I'm* Bob Bicker. My friend, Jake, would like to meet you!"

"Fuck off," said the blond.

Later, Bicker and the Pickleman managed to tie up with a couple of Miss Katie's girls across town at Seo. Bresil. But the girls made an excuse about being sleepy and beat a path to nearby Freaky Pub. Soon after, Bicker and the P'man turned up at Freaky's, too.

"Aha!" yelled the Pickleman, at his subtle best. "Caught you! I *knew* you weren't going home to bed!"

Because of this slight, or because his gherkin fell off that night, the Pickleman wasn't seen around Le Texan for several nights. I saw him sitting outside the Dolphin, throwing suspicious glances, and I honked my horn to catch his attention but, true to character, he looked the wrong way, twice.

* * *

A New Yorker named Jack Ilick struck up a conversation with me at Le Siecle and invited me to lunch. I countered with an invite to a round of brews at the Alamo Bar, and he showed up right after I'd introduced Sara Jane to Googer. Googer riled Sara Jane immediately by criticizing her "one-room schoolhouse" in Funnyville and Sara Jane, recognizing the devil, flashed her rosary beads, earning us all a discourse from Googer on atheism.

I scooted Sara Jane down the bar to Monk and left Googer and Ilick at the bar, bidding satan's work.

Next morning, sitting out in the market place sipping cappucino, Ilick pulled up a seat opposite me.

"I need to get into something," he said. "Do you know of any smuggling going on?"

"Huh? What do you mean?" I asked.

"You know, smuggling. Something I can do here, illegal or whatever." He paused and I said nothing. "Also, I'd like to get new papers. Know where I can go?"

"What kind of papers?"

"French working papers maybe. It doesn't matter. New ID."

"You mean a new name?"

"Yeah, you got it."

"I guess you're not planning to return to New York."

"Nah. Better I don't. I think I'll stick around. But I'm gonna need new ID. Know where I can go?"

Was I being set up? 'Look, I know you like quirky characters,' said a voice belonging to my guardian angel. 'The Pickleman and Crazy George are one thing. Googer's another. But this guy is *evil*. Serious bad news.'

"I think you've come to the wrong town," I told Ilick. "You shouldn't even be *thinking* the words smuggle, illegal and false ID in Monaco. It could be you'd be better off in Italy."

"I kind of like it here," said Ilick. "I think I'm gonna

kick back for a while. Googer says he's got an empty apartment I can use for cheap. Know where I can find any hookers?"

"I really think you'd be better off some place else."

"I thought I saw a hooker up at the casino," said Ilick. "She latched onto me when I was winning. But then I drank too much and lost it all."

With his sleazy moustache, wiry frame and cunning smile, Ilick looks like a Manhattan hot dog vendor who commutes to Atlantic City on weekends. God knows how *he* got past Carabinieri Control.

25

Prince Albert must have heard that the rival Spinolas are using Funnyville U to re-take the Principality. He took a raincheck on the honorary degree they wanted to award him, but did turn up, *sans* Shorty, to hand out degrees to 24 graduates from 14 countries.

Crazy George *didn't* show; was whispered to be on a rampage, cracking down on the jet-setting undergrads and urging them to "get real," an improbable task in Monaco. He flunked most of his pupils, then said, "No more Mister Nice Guy next term." That's Crazy George. One night he's breathing helium and squeaking like Mickey Mouse in front of Princess Caroline on Le Texan's terrace; next morning he's locking his classroom door at nine sharp, refusing entry to tardy students. Some say George flipped when he realized he'd spent 30 grand on partying in six months, half of it on champagne at Jimmy'z, most of it on credit. His synthesizer arrived by boat from the States and now he stays home, whacking his instrument in the wee hours.

Hootenanny George, Miss Katie's left-hand man, walked away with an MBA, though it didn't do him much good at Le Texan. Miss Katie was once mesmerized by Hootenanny's psychic abilities; cherished his computer-produced astrological readings. So Hootenanny spent over a year in the kitchen, decorating plates with guacamole and sour cream, relishing his role as house mystic. Then Miss Katie brought him up front, made him cashier and positioned him next to General Custer for all to see. Monk took a whiff and pronounced him "not a restaurant person," for all to hear. That was enough for Ma Kelly, already irked by Hootenanny's claim that her late best friend, Princess Grace, is his spiritual guide.

Ma Kelly connived with Monk, worked at Kate, and edged poor Hootenanny out of a piece of the place into inevitable unemployment in a state where unemployment is only okay if you are filthy rich.

* * *

The Pickleman and I stood at the bar, next to the cactus, and eyed the unearthly spectacle of Isaac Tigrett's friends, scattered throughout Le Texan to celebrate the imminent wedding of Isaac and Maureen. I was unnerved, but couldn't immediately pin down why; the P'man was just plain disgusted. He hates rock music with a passion, and this extends to rock musicians and fans. Even though Isaac's name and news of the upcoming nuptials had been buzzing around the joint for months, the Pickleman was, as usual, oblivious, and I had to lay it out for him.

"Ever heard of the Hard Rock Cafe?" I asked.

"I wouldn't go into a place with a name like that. Damn rock 'n' roll. First it destroyed jazz, then it ruined three generations of youth, brainwashed them. Disgusting.

"I was once offered a job bodyguarding George Harrison, after that other Beatle got shot, what's his name? Lennon. I turned it down flat. How can you protect someone if you'd just as soon see them dead? I've got principles, you know. If someone wanted to shoot him, I'd step aside and say 'be my guest.' And Mick Jagger. Yecchhh! He's another one. With those big lips, what a target—Blam!— now let's see you play the guitar, Stone!"

The rock 'n' rollers were starting to throw mean glances in our direction; prudence compelled me to change the subject.

"Have you made peace with Monk yet?"

"I'll let him serve me. But first I want to see him in a cowboy hat on a horse. Yeah, that would be a sight." There was no stopping the P'man on this night as he chuckled in appreciation of his own wit, then grew serious and spouted off about the "Texas mafia" that runs Le Texan. "Texans are very clannish. Kate would give a job to Frankenstein if he walked through the door and said he was from Texas."

The way Isaac sauntered in to join his party, you'd think a pop star or a prince had arrived. He tries to mask the extremely high opinion he has of himself with a facade of polyester modesty.

The former burger king has become a crusader for environmental issues. You try to talk with him about it and he hits you with "Mother Theresa" and "the Dalai Llama" and follows with profundities that his entourage eat up like starving Ethiopians.

"Yeah, man, the planet's got only 10 years left."

"Ohhh, nooo. What are we gonna doooo?"

"Yeah, man, the ozone layer."

"Ahhh!"

Isaac is on a mission from God. "I'm blessed to help save the planet," he says, believing this because his Indian guru, Ali Baba or Bibi or something, told him so. That's also why he dresses only in black. Guru guidance. Maureen follows suit, and contrasts her funereal get-up with a milky pale face and unkempt hairdo. Add pointy shoulder pads and the result is Morticia's elder sister from the Addams Family.

Rock Brynner, son of Yul, was skulking around, looking like Lon Chaney, and though Dan Ackroyd didn't show as expected, his sidekick stuntman did—a little bald guy with one eye, a tiny moustache and a small black beret. Uncle Fester.

The Pickleman was nervous. It wasn't Halloween or a CIA reunion, so why all the spooks? Even Googer looked like St. Christopher compared to these fiends.

A witch at a table near the bar kept glancing up at the Pickleman and me, and weird things began to happen. I accidentally slammed my bottle of brew into an empty glass and smashed it into a hundred pieces. Another glass shattered nearby. Then a waitress tripped and nearly broke her neck. But nothing could beat what happened next: the gonads on the Alamo Bar mascot began to contort and ooze a thick black blood.

"They're killing it!" I yelled at Pickleman. It confirmed everything he thought was true about rock 'n' roll, and he booked before the witch could snap a photo and paste it onto a voodoo doll.

Seeing the poor cactus bleed was enough for me and Sara Jane, too. She went for her rosary beads while I searched out garlic and, I swear to God, as soon as she plucked them from her purse, the witch paid her bill and fled like a rat.

Isaac strolled the Alamo Bar, king of kool, engaging in small talk and saying "I'm blessed" to do this and "I'm blessed" to do that. Blessed by Ali Baba or Bibi or something. Yeah, Isaac, like nuke the whales, man.

Then he dragged Miss Katie to the doorway separating

the outdoor terrace from the Alamo Bar. He told her the terrace lighting, the kind that makes bad skin look like a rosy complexion, was all wrong.

"Look inside," he ordered. "Now out. Now in. Now out." Christ, he was trying to twist her head 360 degrees like that horrible scene in *The Exorcist!*

"Look in. Now out. In. Out." Isaac persisted. "See what I mean? It's all wrong!"

"It looks okay to me," said Kate, with a shrug.

"It's *my* opinion that it's all wrong," said Isaac.

"Well, everyone has their own opinion," said Kate sweetly.

"It's *my* opinion that counts." God hath spoken...or was it satan?

Because deep within that super-cool exterior, I sense a Jack Nicholson *Devils of Eastwick* soul. Something about his eyes; something *behind* those eyes...something about all his friends...they were acting as though they'd come *not* for a wedding, but for a *sacrifice*. First, they nail the poor cactus. Next thing, they'll be slaughtering a French poodle on the bar.

They had the wedding anyway, a good cover for all the black magic. None of the invited stars showed—just a couple of burned-out meteorites, and Prince Albert for picture-taking.

In between the extravagant lunches and dinners at Villa Mimosa and Hotel de Paris, coven members took to Le Texan and, as the black magic brigade threw back potions and dreamt up nightmares, the Monaco Cool crowd fingered rosary beads and whispered prayers.

26

"**E**nough is enough," my wife and daughter announced in unison. They weren't talking about my late nights "doing research" at Le Texan, nor my fascination for the likes of Googer or the Mad Market Man. This was more serious than that. "We want a television!"

I went out and bought one, almost a thousand bucks for a 20-inch color set, a hefty price to pay for mass hypnosis.

All you get are five measly channels: three French, one Italian and a local Monte Carlo station. The most popular programs are "The Streets of San Francisco" and, of course, "I Dream of Jeannie." That's the bad news. The good news is that "Roseanne" is at least 10 years away. The best programs are the suntan oil commercials, featuring topless models and signaling the start of the topless season. For months, the only boobs on the beaches in Nice and Menton (never Monaco) are Algerian street peddlers, but by spring, there is real good reason for taking a Sunday stroll on the promenade. Everywhere you look, they stare you in the face; they *reach out* to you: big, round melons, riping for all to see beneath the noonday sun.

Monte Carlo's public beach is cove-shaped. Little open-

air cafés dot the seafront, and this is where you sit, a plea-
sant position on the promenade, sipping pastis, watching
the best in boobery bounce by.

The water looks as clean as a Maine stream as it ripples
gently along the pebbled shore. Not even the sea makes
waves in Monaco. But the aqua-blue translucence disguises
a high bacteria count. The French make an effort to keep
their beaches clean, but Italy mucks them up. Show the
Italians a beach and they'll lay a pipe.

The Pickleman told me this stems from the upper-class
Italian disinterest in beaches and tanning. Imagine a bald
Ichabod Crane in a black bikini brief, half baked, with a
splash of white goop on his long, narrow nose. That's how
the Pickleman looks, lounging back in his deck chair, ramrod straight, his little gherkin barely denting the tight swim-
suit.

"The Italians have the dirtiest water in the Mediterranean," said the P'man. "They don't believe in sunning
themselves. They rate skin color the way Brits rate accents.
The darker your pigment, the more provincial you are. The
patrician types in northern Italy do everything they can to
remain pale-faced. That's the look. Tall, narrow face and
white as a ghost. They want to look as different as possible
from their bumpkin cousins in southern Italy."

The Pickleman stays slim by running every day. Well, he
jogs. No, I guess he walks. But he walks in such a way as
to give the impression he's running, like Lee Majors in "Six
Million Dollar Man." You see him doing this on the promenade, in pickle-green deck shoes and matching tee-shirt.
It's the only time he's not ramrod straight. Because when
he runs, he stoops over like a hermit crab, and even his
knees, buckled low in a halting gait, give him a gastropodic
semblance.

You see no obesity, except for American tourists. Everyone else subscribes to the Monaco Cool diet: eat less, walk more. Restaurants assist by serving itty-bitty portions; the topography obliges by providing hills and steps to climb. The Pickleman, a case in point, subsists on cheese. I almost passed out the first time I caught a whiff of his overripe Camembert, reeking from a *supermarche* bag in the Dolphin.

* * *

Standing on my wrought-iron balcony outside Le Siecle's room 41, I saw Miss Katie waving up at me from the train station below. It was raining, a thin drizzle, and she was standing on the platform beneath a sign that says "Direction Nice." We were too far from each other to communicate, so we blew kisses as the westward-bound train rolled in. It was 6pm, an hour before Le Texan opens and, wherever Kate was headed it didn't feel like she was coming back. Her authority eroded by Isaac and Monk, I knew she'd been thinking of taking off, opening a place of her own without the stress of a family business. Could this be goodbye?

There was no Katie at Le Texan that night and I was afraid to ask where she'd gone. And I realized a whole generation of Miss Katie's girls had passed. And no Alamo Bar mascot...no Alamo Bar mascot? I nearly panicked. It wasn't on the bar. Those damn witches must have bled the poor cactus to death!

"Rich!" I yelled. "The mascot?"

Richie read the desperation in my eyes. "It's okay, don't worry," he said. "Out on the terrace."

Relieved, I went to inspect the cactus, recuperating

from the sorceror's spell. One gonad was completely deflated.

I ordered a brew, took a swig and nearly spewed it across the bar when I saw what the fiends had done to General Custer. A warlock had stuck the stem of a black rose into a fracture on the wooden bust, right down to his heart.

The Pickleman walked in at this moment and saw the black rose growing out of Custer's heart.

"Yep, rock 'n' roll," said the P'man. "Rock music is criminal. That wedding must have been a scream. Geddit? Heh, heh. Yeah, funerals can be more fun than weddings."

The Pickleman was no longer playing Tonto to Bob Bicker's Lone Ranger. They fell out after an afternoon's cruising in Bicker's cigarette boat. The P'man had proven to be more a hindrance than a help as a sailor, doing everything requested of him the wrong way. Bicker finally declared that everyone in their party of six would be better served if the P'man did nothing, and the Pickleman snapped. "If you wanted professional sailors to ride with you," he shouted, "you should have asked them!" He left in a huff, refusing an invitation to dinner.

* * *

My wife's sister arrived in town with her husband and we made a cozy foursome out on Le Texan's terrace. Then Googer walked in and, uninvited, pulled up a chair and changed the subject to bare boobs, zeroing in on my sis-in-law's first flicker of disapproval. He followed with a harangue designed to get our ganders up.

"Americans are the stupidest people in the Western world," Googer harped. "And *you're* retarded for not learning French," he said to me. "The French say *oui, oui* and *you* think they're looking for a bathroom."

The Goog's Hungarian girlfriend had abruptly walked out on him a couple of nights earlier. This happens a lot.

It was awfully tempting to whop a beer bottle across his cheshire cat grin, but it was this loss of control that satan begged. So we looked into the eyes of Son of Sam II and laughed; the more we laughed, the more insulting he became, until he couldn't stand the laughter any more and left.

More important than Googer or anything else at Le Texan that night, Miss Katie was back. Googer may be the devil, but Katie's reappearance proved that God is out there, looking after Le Texan and the Monaco Cool.

27

The only Monaco Cool place to meet Prince Albert for the first time is the Alamo Bar. And this is where we were finally introduced by his good buddy Mike, Miss Katie's brother. Monaco revolves around its first family, so everyone aspires to meet and socialize with its members. The result is an endless competition to see who can score the brownest nose.

I was still hungover and glassy-eyed from the night before, champagne bubbles searching for new ways to escape my intestines. It had been a good night's drinking; a bad morning's waking up. We'd been out to see the *Folie Russe*—a topless floorshow at Loews—and finished up partying with a troupe of dancers at a nightclub called The Living Room. When I woke up it felt like they'd been dancing on my head.

We were with Monaco's coolest couple: Clay, a good ole boy from Arkansas, and Stephanie, from California, who dances in the *Russe*.

Ice buckets of champagne surrounded us at The Living Room and Shorty, hoping to indulge, approached Stephanie.

"Hi Shorty!" Steph hollered, accidentally, and then embarrassed, continued, "Uh, I mean, how ya doin' ya big dude!" Shorty was not amused.

While I was quaffing bubbly, Ma Kelly was tearing into Googer a mile away. It came back to me from three eye-witnesses.

Googer had walked into Le Texan amid a rush on the place, no reservation, and ordered Tony to fix him table.

"You can kiss mah ass," grumbled Tony.

So the Goog grabbed a chair and, uninvited, plunked himself at Ma Kelly's *table d'honneur*. I'd told Kelly that very afternoon about Googer's gall and she intuitively knew who he was.

Tony came up from behind to point him out with an obscene arm gesture, but this proved unnecessary.

"Look at the asshole I got stuck with!" boomed Ma Kelly, pointing at Googer, two feet away.

"Hmmm. He's some asshole all right," said Tony.

Googer froze, in shock. A waitress stopped by the table and he ordered a glass of wine to calm his nerves; the Goog hardly ever drinks.

"Make sure that sonofabitch has his own bill!" hollered Ma Kelly. "*I'm* not paying for his wine!"

Googer sat like a mouse, drank a few sips of wine, then left quietly without a peep.

I'd seen Googer once in between the night he harassed my foursome and Kelly dealing him Texan-style justice. He approached me at the Alamo Bar and held up a hardcover book, *French for Beginners*.

"This is for you," he said, and he held out the book.

Aha, I thought, a peace offering, and I flipped through the pages, pleased I hadn't told him to fuck himself.

"Ten bucks," said Googer.

"What?"

"The book costs ten bucks."

"Go fuck yourself." I handed back the book.

Googer let it pass. It had been a good day. He had closed a deal on a *viager*.

"A what?"

"*Viager*. It means you give an old person some money, a third of what their home is worth, and when they croak, the home is yours."

"You *are* the fucking devil."

"No, no, no. It's common practice here. It allows older people who need money to continue to live in their home instead of having to sell it."

"So you're subsidizing an old-age pensioner?"

"Yeah. She's 85. A widow. The statistics are against her."

"What if she lives to be a hundred?"

"Nah. I looked in her bathroom cabinet. It's full of medicine."

* * *

"What do you like, boy, champag-na?"

This is what the Chiliman says to me every morning outside his Condamine Café, to which I had defected from the Dolphin and Lyin' Leon.

Before you even stirred your sugar, Leon would plop down opposite and start babbling about the 189 million he lost in Iran—"I'm gonna sue!" he hollers, growing indignant, a well-rehearsed routine, and then he babbles some more about this currency, that currency, his Saab Turbo and a host of other things you don't want to hear about at eight in the morning. He concludes each new topic by rising in his seat, and you think, "The Lord does have mercy, he's leaving!" But all he does is shift himself, probably to pass gas, and settle into a more comfortable position from which to continue his tirade.

"Hey Chiliman," I say, "just cook me one of your caps of cino and don't be sassy!"

The Chiliman calls everyone "boy." I took him to Le Texan once and he wrankled Richie by ordering, "Gimme anudder Mezcal, *boy*!" Then he took one bite of chicken nachos and pushed the plate away.

"Something wrong?" asked Richie.

"No, *boy*, 'cept dis testes lak sheet."

Then Chiliman got down to some serious Mezcal drinking, the kind with a worm floating in the bottle, nearly blew his doughnuts on the Alamo Bar and had to be rolled down to his tiny houseboat at the port.

* * *

And so I finally met Prince Albert, near where he carved his Texan nickname—"Al-bop"—into the sculptured mural of the Alamo.

Prince Albert tools around town in a sporty white Beamer. His two bodyguards follow discreetly in a drab Peugeot, and when they lose their royal charge, they head for Le Texan and wait. Shorty, too, though Shorty's harder to lose. He paces the bar, repeating "I'm waiting for *him*, I'm waiting for *him*," over and over again.

Behind the bar, Prince Albert's cousin Richie shakes and pours, whipped into a fine specimen of barkeep by Monk—and more experienced in foreign affairs than Henry Kissinger.

But even with its royal seal of approval, you could still feel the sun setting on the wild spirit of Le Texan. Under Miss Katie's stewardship, the joint broke all the rules; its Western lawlessness struck enough gold to support the character richness that clings to the place like algae to a Venice wharf.

Isaac and Monk talk incessantly about "systems" and "structured procedures" and "turning tables," and Miss Katie was just too overworked to fight back.

An old wagon wheel on the terrace was banished to the basement, more room for another chair. Gone, too, were the baskets of tortilla chips and salsa that garnished the bar, compliments of the house. Some regulars were whispering that the portions had shriveled.

Crazy George hadn't been by in three weeks. The Swede stopped coming; something to do with his dog not being welcome, in a country where dogs are sacred.

And it seemed only a matter of time before the Pickleman would be discouraged from occupying a stool for half the night to sip *vin rouge*.

28

It was a radical night at Le Texan. Monk was parading around the bar with a star-shaped sheriff's badge pinned to his *chemise*. It was engraved with "Santa Fe," which I mistook from a distance as "Shirley," and a new nickname was born.

Shorty was with another little guy, Weasel Eyes, who bills himself as an independent film packager; residue, no doubt, from Cannes. Shorty was pitching a deal, dishing up Prince Albert's name as a kind of collateral, and attempting to tackle a big, fat Havana. He lit up, puffed, turned purple, gagged and tried to keep a straight face. Even Tony, busy waiting tables, caught the act, and walked by Sara Jane and I, shaking his head. "Did you see Shorty, smoking that cee-gar?" he hooted. "She-et, it bigger than he is!"

Then Shorty approached Ma Kelly's table to pay homage to the matriarch and Kelly tore into him, just like she had done to the Goog.

"Why don't you call me anymore?" asked Shorty.

"I've *never* called you," said Kelly. "Why should I start now?"

It went downhill from there. Shorty announced that his wife would arrive in a few weeks for a reconciliation and Kelly asked, with a hoot, if it would interfere with a relationship he'd just begun with a 17 year-old junior at the American School in Nice.

The Pickleman, appearing for the first time in four nights, took his usual position next to General Custer. He likes military people.

"I was actually on my way to a party," said the Pickleman, "but I got the dates mixed up." He watched Monk intently as Sheriff Shirley swaggered around, looking as though he owned the place. "I ignore him," said the P'man. "He *hates* that."

"Maybe it's time to bury the hatchet," I said.

Monk, aware of the Pickleman's attention, cupped his hands round his mouth and whispered "Wrong-way Yennie" in our direction, but the P'man was oblivious.

"No thanks," said the Pickleman. "I'm not fucking gregarious. Who needs it? First I want to see him on a horse—can you imagine that? Heh, heh. Then I'll stop ignoring him."

Crazy George was back, three nights in a row.

But the main reason Le Texan was rad was the Alamo Bar mascot. It was back on the bar.

* * *

Ma Kelly telephoned Shorty the next morning with an apology.

"I thought you were my friend?" whined Shorty.

"I have no business making judgments about your personal life and for that I'm sorry," said Kelly. "But maybe you could be more discreet since you're behind the Prince so much."

"I'm a *good* influence on Albert," protested Shorty. "I'm trying to get rid of the riffraff around him."

Ma Kelly was speechless, a condition that does not befall her often.

"People like Fat Antonio," continued Shorty in earnest. "I take care of Albert."

* * *

Le Texan was beat the next night; devoured whole by the table-turners, system structurers and the see-and-be-seeners that belong in Monte Carlo. Yuks like Sylvia Panass (short for "pain-in-the-ass"), self-appointed queen of the foreign residents who started a newsletter as an outlet for her appalling poetry. Worse, the Alamo Bar mascot was demoted again, usurped by an avant-garde sculpture of a gay Indian on a horse.

"The hell with this," I said to Sara Jane. "Let's get our sheep together and get the flock outta here."

We took off to Funnyville, to an English-style pub called the Flag and Castle. The *maison blanc*, from Alsace, sweetened the emotional trauma enveloping my soul over Le Texan for no rational reason. We ventured out to reconnoiter the new cafés, bars and restaurants that speckle the winding port and...lo and behold, was that the Pickleman standing at the bar in a cozy joint called La Regata? Yes, yes, yes! We joined him, and after he got over the shock, we felt like three Russian defectors exchanging notes on the new world.

Behind the bar, Colleen from California poured a round of vino. She and her boyfriend, Mad Max, an Italian Monegasque, tend bar, and Max's mother grills a tasty *croque monsieur*.

It was near midnight, and we all sat out on the terrace, a lit candle on the table, sipping wine and savoring the clear view of Ventimiglia beyond the water, contrasted by the stark cliff face of the Rock, crowned by the Cathedral de Notre Dame where Princess Grace was married and buried, its golden lights aglow beneath a star-filled sky.

Suddenly, the Wind Spirit, a cruise ship with four large, computerized masts, glided into view, its billowy sails illuminated by bright colored lights as it disembarked from Monaco's port into the night. A salt breeze wafted in over the berthed boats, bobbing in the port. And Stephen Bishop on Riviera Radio singing "On and On."

At precisely midnight, the cathedral lights high above switched off, and Sara Jane and I started back down the port. At a restaurant called The Off Shore, we found them, more defectors. Sitting around a rectangular table on the terrace: Prince Albert, Shorty, and his riffraff gang, including Weasel Eyes and Fat Antonio.

29

Hootenanny George took me to lunch at the Chiliman's café. We got talking about Le Texan, and my line about free-spirit anarchism versus structured systems hit home.

"I like the place because of the statement it made," I told George. "The revolution starts here."

"I'm glad you said that," murmured George. "I'm not the only one."

Miss Katie, Tony, and Hootenanny George were at Le Texan from its conception. They collectively made the place a huge success by injecting their personalities, along with their hearts and souls, 15 hours a day. When those only peripherally involved saw gold dust in the pan, they called the mining techniques obsolete and ordered new technology.

Inside the original Hard Rock Cafe in London there is a framed photograph, prominently hung, of a smiling, bewhiskered Isaac Tigrett with the caption, "Our Founder." Some might say Isaac's ex-partner Peter Morton was the real brains behind Hard Rock; certainly he was a *co-founder*. Isaac and Peter stopped talking in the '70s, finally divorced and the Mississippi River became their border.

It burned me up that this *un*-Monaco Cool pseud had designs on my favorite watering hole.

"It's the little things," I told George. "The subtleties."

"What little things?"

"The Alamo Bar mascot. The wagon wheel." I felt foolish for a second. Until I saw George's eyes begin to water a tinge.

"That was Kate's wheel," said George, brushing at his right eye. "Just before opening, everyone wanted to get rid of the wheel, but Kate said, 'I want a wagon wheel on my terrace'..."

George loves those people, loves the place. Maybe he's *not* a restaurant person, but it was combination of personalities, the human chemistry, that brought to life, here and now, an Edouard Cortes painting. And Goddamit, people have got to be more important than systems.

I gave the Alamo Bar a miss for a couple nights and went to Max and Colleen's place in Funnyville.

Then came Le Texan's anniversary bash; one year old. I got there early. Mike, decked out in ostrich cowboy boots and matching ostrich belt with a large, oval-shaped silver buckle, helped set tables. Mike is one of the world's nicest guys; a born baby kisser. He's all over the place, pumping palms, pecking cheeks, eyes everywhere at once, checking out who's coming and who's going. You can hear him whisper to sister Kate, "What's that guy's name?" and, sufficiently informed, greet the patron like a long-lost cousin.

Miss Katie was all dolled up in black and red lizard cowboy boots, a red denim cowboy shirt, shoulders cut away to expose peaches and cream flesh, a large rhinestone brooch that said "Rodeo" and rhinestone earrings in the shape of Texas. If the Lone Star State had its own Statue of Liberty, it would be Miss Katie.

Jim Bowie and Davy Crockett would have been proud

of the Alamo Bar. John Wayne, as always, was peering through an Alamo window, shotgun at the ready. And the Lone Star flag, sculpted out of a petrified paper napkin, shone brightly beneath the small spotlights that illuminate the bar and its magnificent Alamo backdrop.

It was the Monaco Cool version of the Red Cross Ball, blue jeans instead of tuxedos and gowns.

Richie and Tony churned out buckets of margaritas for the collective unquenchable thirst. The Pickleman was throwing them back with dispatch.

"Someone missing?" the P'man bellowed at me from across the room, a shit-faced grin from ear to ear.

Monk, Sheriff Shirley, wasn't at the party; nor Isaac, though Maureen put in an appearance, looking like Princess Momby in *Return to Oz*.

Prince Albert arrived and was immediately besieged by fartlickers, including Shorty, whom Albert appeared to ignore. Shorty looked perplexed, sweating pellets; aware, perhaps, that his days as Prince Albert's fishmonger were numbered.

Crazy George made a dozen pitches for a schtoink, and even the Swede made an appearance.

Round about midnight I had a mad craving for La Regata, and, with the bash winding down, Sara Jane and I spread the word that we were taking the party with us.

We told the Pickleman first. He checked his watch and said, "I don't know about that. Max and Colleen lock up early on Sunday. And anyway you can't do that. That's *my* place!"

Miss Katie overheard.

"What's this Regata business?" she demanded. "Are you cheatin' on me?"

"The old magic has disappeared," I said.

Miss Katie pulled the toy pistol from her belt. "All right!" she hollered. "I'm gonna fix that Colleen once and for all!"

Sara Jane and I set off and discovered La Regata was locked up tighter than the Pickleman's bikini brief. We took position in the open-air at the Flag and Castle, two terraces away.

Within minutes, the Pickleman came stumbling along. He cursed loudly when he saw La Regata was closed, and he peered through the darkened window, figuring we'd given him the slip.

"Over here, Jake!" I waved.

The Pickleman looked the wrong way. I had to call out twice more. He weaved over, bounced off a five-foot neon ice cream cone and almost tripped over a chair. Then he looked up and realized we were outside the Flag and Castle.

"I fucking *hate* this place!" screamed the Pickleman. "That's the last time I listen to a civilian. Goddamit! I thought you knew something I didn't!"

"Sit down, Jake," I said. "I want to congratulate you. This is the first time you've been right about something."

Then I broke into uproarious laughter. Partly because I had drunk too many margaritas and partly because the P'man had drunk too many margaritas. I doubled up in convulsions.

"I hope you're laughing with me and not *at* me," said the Pickleman in the most solemn voice he could muster.

I hit the deck, tears streaming down my face. The Pickleman is the funniest straight man in the world.

"And you're drinking fucking *water*," said the P'man, pointing at my bottle of Perrier.

"HA! HA! HA!" These were full belly laughs, the healthiest in the world.

"It's been a great night," said the Pickleman. "I got to cuddle with Kate and someone took a picture of us. I can't wait to see that picture."

"HAW, HAW, HAW...Oh, God...HA! HA! HA!..."

I finally calmed down and went for my notebook.

"I want five percent every time my name comes up," said the Pickleman.

This started me up again, slapping my knee, pounding my fist on the table and hooting uncontrollably.

A waitress came out to take our order.

"This one's on me," said the Pickleman. He hadn't bought anyone a drink since 1966. "Give them anything they want, as long as it's cheap," he said, meaning every word.

I was going nuts. "HA HA HA HA—Owwweeee!"

A convoy of party-makers pulled alongside, but it was too late for Funnyville, and they U-turned and sped off to Jimmy'z.

"Want to come to my place for a nightcap?" asked the Pickleman.

Sara Jane and I looked at each other in disbelief. The Pickleman's inner sanctum?

It was a small studio apartment. The P'man's bookshelves had warped beneath the weight of spy thrillers. Side tables displayed ancient Greek artifacts; tribal spears poked out from nooks; native aborigine masks decorated the walls.

The Pickleman uncorked a bottle of *rouge* and asked if we would like to hear some Russian folk music. "This is the real thing," he said. "KGB music."

He slipped the LP from its tattered cover, plopped it on the phonograph and joined us out on the terrace.

The KGB music was loud. It sounded peculiar, like a pack of munchkins singing.

"Isn't this music too fast?" I finally asked.

The Pickleman jumped up and changed the speed from 33 to 45 RPMs.

"Damn KGB!" cursed the Pickleman. "You can't trust the bastards!"

But by this time, nearly 2am, it wasn't only the P'man who was cursing. About 30 of his neighbors had awakened and they were hurling a cacophony of abuse in our direction, in at least five different languages. The Pickleman was oblivious to the attention.

"I think you'd better turn down the KGB, Jake," I said.

"Fuck 'em!" said the P'man. "I only do this once a year."

30

"Remember Jack Nicholson in *One Flew Over the Cuckoo's Nest*? He was wild, fun to be with, brimming with enthusiasm and totally out of control." I was talking to Miss Katie over cappucino at the Chiliman's café. "That's kind of like what you created at Le Texan. But remember at the end of the flick, after Nicholson had a lobotomy? That's where Le Texan is going."

Miss Katie had asked for my observations, and there was no point in being less than candid.

"They're trying to snatch the place from you, chip away at your authority until you're so frustrated, your morale so low that you walk."

A day earlier, Kate had issued her family with an ultimatum: Let me run the joint my way or I'll leave and start my own restaurant.

"You're playing right into Isaac Tigrett's hands," I told her. "That's exactly what he wants. You're the last hurdle before he can call the place *home*. If you take a hike, the Alamo Bar belongs to Sheriff Shirley and Ali Baba, Bibi or something."

"We put a lot into Le Texan," Kate reflected. "More than a year of tender loving care. It *would* be difficult to leave."

"You shouldn't even *think* of leaving," I told her. "You *are* Le Texan. Davy Crockett didn't surrender the Alamo. Why should you? You have to stay and fight, for yourself, for Le Texan, and for Monaco Cool. Seize back the authority they've chipped away."

Monk had just flown home to Dallas, but was planning to return two weeks hence to rule the roost behind the Alamo Bar.

"Your place isn't big enough for the two of you," I said. "Monk's an awfully nice sheriff and, personally, I like him. But the chemistry is all wrong.

"You know why the Swede doesn't come in anymore, don't you? He couldn't understand why you wouldn't tell him yourself."

"Tell him what?"

"To leave his dog at home."

"*I* didn't know that!" said Katie. "Me and Tony used to say, 'move that darn dog out of the way—coming through!'"

"Yeah, that's the old, pre-lobotomized Le Texan. Nobody minded that kind of talk, they thrived on it as part of the freewheeling atmosphere. But you know what really worries me? That if I walk into Le Texan in five years, there's going to be a photograph of Isaac on the wall, with a caption that says 'Our Founder.'"

Miss Katie was ready to defend the Alamo.

And with the school year coming to a close, and America calling my name, I was ready to call it a wrap. It was time to return to reality, to search for Bedford Falls. You can take only so much perfection. And, anyway, Monaco truly *isn't* a family place; the temptations are enormous and tattletales on every street corner.

Another consideration: If I stayed even a month

longer, it would become difficult for my daughter to re-adjust from birthday celebrations aboard yachts to parties with Ronald McDonald. Talk about culture shock.

The turnover in Monaco among foreign residents is rapid and dramatic, and after less than a year I was practically a veteran. Lynn the assistant barkeep, a founding member of Miss Katie's girls, was back in New Zealand; others were making plans to make tracks. A new crowd was already taking over. Better I join the Monaco Cool in Exile than grow stale.

Part of the expatriate dilemma is you get awfully mixed up, like trying to reconcile a Brooks Brothers appearance with an anarchistic state of mind. You long for a rocking chair, a fireplace and a wrap-around porch, a yellow schoolbus and smiling neighbors who borrow sugar; Halloween and Thanksgiving, and being able to buy a lightbulb without a two-minute game of charades with a stock clerk. That's on even days. On odd days you want to be challenged by a menu, hit Loew's Spa, Café de Paris, Le Texan and mix it up with Miss Katie, Crazy George, Pickleman and even Shorty's riffraff gang. Because you know in your heart that once you cross 34 it takes living abroad to have the kind of gang from *St. Elmo's Fire* that you had in high school and a world that feels fresh and alive. You make your friends in school, in the service and among expats. Almost everyone else is an acquaintance.

My throat felt dry and lumpy as I packed up room 41 at Le Siecle and took a final look out the window, up at the *Tet de Chien* and down at the train station. It had been a magical year; deep down, I already knew I was destined to remember it as one of the best of my life.

I bid Monsieur Molass farewell and he told me that Ilick, the sleazy hot dog vendor, had skipped town. All

Molass lost was the price of an unpaid lunch. It was Googer who got honched good. Ilick owed the hostile Hungarian 300 bucks' rent, and the Goog went bananas in Molass's lobby when his ex-tenant did not keep an appointment to settle the tab.

* * *

I took my last stand at Le Texan next to General Custer at the Alamo Bar.

Miss Katie bounded over, defiant, radiating renewed spirit. Pinned to her denim blouse was a round badge that said: "Ask me about my lobotomy." The old wagon wheel was out on the terrace.

Then I noticed a sign behind the bar, normally used to promote cocktail specials, but on this night proclaiming, "Robie, you promised."

I leaned over to Hootenanny George, behind the cash register. "What's that all about?"

"Don't you remember?" asked George.

"Remember what?"

"You promised on your last night you'd have an upside-down margarita."

"I can't do it," I pleaded. "Too many meals out, too much wine. My stomach is already spasmodic."

"Sorry," Richie chimed in. "A promise is a promise. I heard it, too."

"Oh, shit."

The Chiliman joined me next to General Custer. We popped open a couple cans of Tezcate and drank them the Chiliman's way, out of the can with lime juice and salt spread liberally around the pop-top hole.

Miss Katie grabbed a pair of stetsons off Custer and

plopped them on Cosilito and me, and the Chiliman hooted a Mexican whoop so awesome, even Custer grunted approval.

"I don't know what we're gonna do without you around," said Miss Katie.

"I don't know what *I'm* gonna do without me around!"

The Pickleman walked in, his first public appearance since arousing the wrath of his neighbors with high-decibel KGB music.

"You still alive?" I thought they had dispatched him to Pickle heaven.

"The day after was *not* funny," said the P'man. He watched the Chiliman and I with disdain as we drained our cans and ordered another round of Tezcate.

"Let me tell you about my latest fantasy," said the Pickleman, perking up. "Monk stands at one end of the bar, dressed in black, everything tight-fitting, three sizes too small. And he's facing off with Shorty down the other end of the bar, both ready to draw. Shorty's dressed in white and everything's too big on him, including the cowboy hat—it falls over his eyes. What do you think of that, huh, huh?"

Sara Jane, Clay and Steph, the Chiliman, Pickleman, Tony and Miss Katie gathered 'round. The time had come for an upside-down margarita.

I leaned back on the bar, face up. Hootenanny George tied a bib around my neck. Miss Katie let loose a full-bodied "Whooooeeee!," the Chiliman hooted, a few people whistled, the Pickleman smirked and Richie clambered his bottles of Cuervo Gold, Triple sec and lime juice into position.

"Open wide," said Richie.

"Gurgle, gurgle," was all I could manage as the fastest drink of my life descended down my gullet. And damn, it tasted good!

Gulping an upside-down margarita was easy. What came next was more difficult: saying goodbye.

"I'm really gonna miss you," I told the Pickleman, and I think it was the first time in his life anyone told him that.

"Wait a minute!" hollered Miss Katie. "You can't leave without your goody box!"

"My what?"

Katie reached behind Custer and pulled out a red, white and blue, stars and stripes carrier bag.

"Go on, you have to open it *now*," said Kate.

I popped another Tezcate and reached inside. The first item was a Le Texan tee-shirt, then a mini-photo album with six choice pics. A Heineken bottle cap and a shot glass, a matchbox and a vinyl horse, cut out from a place mat and signed by the staff.

The last item was a card with handwritten inscriptions from the Monaco Cool crowd. I couldn't read it there without betraying serious emotion.

Tony and I exchanged bear hugs. "Miss Katie's damn lucky to have a shotgun like you, dude. Watch her back."

"Y'all come back, y'hear?" said Tony, and when that man smiles, happiness radiates a hundred yards.

Then Miss Katie and I embraced. "I think I'll miss you most of all," I said. We held on to each other.

Do you know how Dorothy Gale of Kansas felt when she said goodby to Scarecrow, Tin Woodsman, and Cowardly Lion? I do. I found out when I said goodbye to the Monaco Cool gang, my family of rootless, adventure-seeking expats who all needed each other.

In the solitude of my apartment, amid packed cases, the lights of Italy twinkling in the distance, I read the Le Texan farewell card. This is what Miss Katie wrote:

Now if everyone's just gonna up and go
Who's gonna defend the Alamo?
You can count on me to stand tight
Wouldn't leave without putting up a fight
No one's gonna put me up against a Rock

Unless they're in for some future shock
Well, we'll miss your smilin' bearded face
It just won't be the same old magical place
Hurry up and get your notebook and self back
Before this place turns into just another
   organized shack

* * *

When Le Texan opened its doors the next night, I was
halfway across the Atlantic, winging my way "home"
aboard an Air France jumbo.

New York's JFK felt like the pilot had taken a wrong
turn and landed in Lagos, Nigeria. Our driver was late, the
public telephones didn't work and the loitering natives
looked dangerous. We were outside the bubble, like babes
born into the world from a secure womb.

As we wound our way home to the Jersey shore in a
limo, the tinted glass softened a view of Staten Island's
monstrous garbage dumps, and a television distracted us
from the chemical refineries and manufacturing plants that
consume the Jersey landscape from Newark to the Amboys.
I swigged a bottle of Bud and checked my watch: closing
time at Le Texan.